MY MARQUESS

Thiago Helvetica

Contents

D ominic McAllister, The Marquess of Grisham is a tall, dark and handsome bachelor. He is a hedonistic rake in his own right and he prefers to stay that way.

The Rose...

Emilia Westham the tons petite wallflower, a meek, young beauty that has not yet blossomed.

When Dominic finds Emilia injured on his boat, he nurses her back to health and events take place that go beyond his control.

It awakens a passionate encounter that shakes them both to their core.

His tender caresses and stolen kisses turn the petite wallflower into a sensual, beautiful rose that blossoms under his touch.

One he plucks and keeps for himself.

Chapter 1

- -

She stood before the mirror eyeing the dress that was fashioned for her. She was poked, pulled and squeezed to no end. Until it fit her thin form splendidly. Layers and layers of fabric weighed her down and squeezed her uncomfortably, but it was the way of it, the way of societies fashion. She gloomily sighed as her long beautiful chestnut brown hair was tucked and twisted with pins in place in a ridiculous looking hair do that made her shiver with her bare neck exposed. She sadly stood where Sarah her maid left her staring into the great abyss she was drawn into.

The slight reflection of someone behind her brought her back to reality. There he stood leaning against the door jam ogling her. She detested him so much. Stephen her uncle's stepson stood lazily eyeing her with unmistakable lust and she cringed. If not for his blackguard and slimy ways, she would treat him different but she could only look at him with disdain. Her stomach lurched as he leaned back and looked both ways in the halls to see if anyone comes before he entered unceremoniously. Whirling around her eyes clashed with his.

"Get out" she ordered.

Her meek soft voice couldn't deter or scare a mouse.

Stephen cracked a devious smile that pushed her back.

"Come now sweet one, why so angry." his voice teasingly dangerous neared her.

Looking up into his face, she watched his eyes trail hungrily over her well-formed breasts that hid demurely under her snug-fitting bodice with a floral stitch neckline.

Menacing fingers glided along it before she slapped them away. Quickly he pulled her into a breathless embrace as she clawed at his hands and arms; he trailed kisses along her throat and laughed huskily as she cried out to let her go. With a powerful hand, he grabbed the back of her head and kissed her.

Bile grew in her stomach at the taste of brandy and cigar smoke on his breath. Before he could slip his tongue into her mouth, she bit his lip that he let out a curse and howl.

"You bitch!" he hissed.

With speed, she stepped out of his grasp as he lunged for her and ran for the door before he whirled her around. With lightening speed, the palm of her hand landed with a crude thwack across his cheek. Quickly gaining her footing, he grabbed her. The slight footsteps and chatter of Sarah with another maid stiffened his next move.

"Don't worry my sweet, one day I will have you and I only hope it will be soon," he jeered between his teeth.

With that threat, he planted one more forced kiss on her mouth before shoving her aside and storming out of her room nearly knocking over Sarah.

Large eyes peered through the door as they watched Emilia weakly slump to the floor. Running quickly to her side Sarah and Gertrude helped her up. She was in a state of undoing that she felt faint. Quickly they fanned her and helped her to a nearby stoop.

"That evil man did something to you didn't he milady" she cupped Emilia's pale cheeks that slowly regained their color.

"Look at the poor way he left you Lady Emilia" Gertrude crooned offering her a glass of water.

Shaking her head Emilia worried about the fuss and rejected the idea of telling her uncle as they pleaded with her to do so.

"If I tell it would only create a rift between them," she quietly said wiping away a tear.

Her soft voice explained many things to them they did not agree with. She felt an outsider, unwanted and a burden to her uncle ever since she arrived on his doorstep. Her only next of kin took charge of her with hesitance after her parents died in a coach accident. Her mother's only living brother came forward only for duty but not for love she explained. His distant overbearing authoritive ways sometimes clashed with her free willed wayward and mischievous nature.

Rules were set and firmly abided by in his household. Being a Duke, he had to uphold to societies stature and he expected her to do the same. She ached for the old way of her life where she ran free on her grandparent's lands in the Scottish mountains. The way her bare feet caressed the lush green grass. Her long walks in the open clean air. But, as life so meagerly fixed itself for her, those dreams only but memories toyed with her as she was brought before the Ton and their customs.

The uptight haughty lifestyle had no room for such frivolous dalliances. Here in this life it was about courting, marriage, fashion and other worldly things that pertained to man. She was to be courted and placed within a profitable marriage dutifully according to her station. As if placed on the butchering block the more tender morsels of meat were chosen so therefore, she was the meat.

Chapter 2

Morning light gave no promise to how long the sun would hide behind the clouds. Slightly squinting up he watched as one or two clouds drifted by.

Leaning back he was drifting in and out of a sweet slumber as his boat lulled with the waves on the open water.

Taking his early morning boat ride gave him great escape from the stuffy London streets and its people.

Day and night he was goaded into assisting balls, dances and dinners. Stuffed into tight jackets, cravats and surcoats just stifled him. The crisp seawater wafted thru to his nose and it brought a smile on his face.

Eventually he had to get back he breathed he had work to attend to and no one could be left with the task.

He chuckled at his butler Bufford as he followed him to the docks with book and pen in hand delegating and asking questions on estate accounts and what was to be done in his absence. With quick halt, he had to quickly grab the poor duddy old man before he toppled them both into the water.

Rolling his eyes he promised Bufford he would return in a couple of hours and that he was sure in that small amount of time the world would not come to an end with his absence but pretty much rejoice in it.

The baffled stare of Bufford made him grin.

Unfortunately, he must go with that promise and return, if not he would send a search for him most surely.

Quickly standing he rolled up the boats anchor. He let down the sail and let the brisk breeze pull him in the direction he needed to go while he stirred his boat home.

Some hours or so went by before he could see the docks pulling into view.

With an oath under breath and a curse, the small plump view of Bufford stood waving jubilee as he saw the boat pulling in.

"Curses Bufford I asked that you wait for me at home." He yelled from the boat.

His sullen nervous look lowered his eyes as he watches his Lord climb above the dock.

"Aye, forgive me M'lord, but I was a trifle bit worried you were not going to return in time for supper." he stammered pulling his watch from his pocket. The poor old man was indeed growing old he breathed. He has been a loyal butler to his father, a gentleman's, gentleman as you would call he was and continued so until his father's passing and still serving him.

By mid-morning, she was in her uncle's music room on the piano practicing her lessons with Madam Georgette. The tunes spilled softly from each key once or twice an off-key sound would escape only to have a long thin stick briskly tap her hands.

"Sit up straight Emilia, if you would sit properly and stop clawing at the keys you can play with finesse" the goading high pitched voice ridiculed her endlessly so she began to detest the lessons, the instructor and the piano altogether.

"Forgive Me Madam." She squeezed her fingers together before turning her attentions back to the black and ivory keys.

"My goodness Emilia, sit straight before you slump to the floor." The familiar voice of Joanna her older sister rang out. She stiffened at her voice entering from the hall into the music room. Stopping to halt on the last note she stroke, she blew a breath at her sister's criticism. Turning on the oak bench, she watched her sister remove her cloak and gloves.

Joanna was older than her by five or six years, she was haughty with an air of supremacy towards her. She rather developed a closeness of some sort with her after her parents died. Joanna chose to live with her Aunt Matilda in Gloucester and would visit often to attend the local social events. Ever so often would visit and she would sit with her and talk very little, but as if she strained to force herself to do so.

Although they were from the same father, they had little similarities. Where Joanna had blonde hair with blue eyes and was tall and skinny with a long neck, she on the other hand was petite in stature, slender with chestnut brown hair that spilled down her back and green eyes. Like her mother as her grandfather would say.

She watched as Joanna handed her cloak and gloves to Jeoffry their butler before strolling over to her and giving her a kiss on each cheek. Fake! Nevertheless, it was bearable. She pulled her up to her feet and twirled her around. With satisfaction splaying on her lips, she smiled.

"I do say you look very lovely sister." She smiled.

Emilia not use to hearing such flattering words from Joanna ducked her head coyly and thanked her.

Pulling her close to sit beside her on a chair nearby, she looked skeptically at Johanna because she rarely ever did this.

"Tell me, sister, are you going to attend the Van Camps Soiree? I hear it will be a splendid event." Her eyes twinkled with the news.

Lowering her head, she honestly did not want to attend. She grew tiresome of the London season and the gossip, although interesting was all they did at those events.

"I suppose I am. If you are going, uncle will insist that I go along as well." Emilia sighed.

It was the talk of the evening of Lady VanCamps dinner party a must go to affair. She returned from France and brought with her a dashing gentleman friend. Soon, perhaps husband number three as some teetered and gasped with gossip. Most went for the food and music, others went for the gossip to see who came with who. Such things were dull for Emilia but a must for her sister and Aunt Matilda who was scandalously the biggest gossiper of the ton. She was out right forced to go. She dreaded these affairs and it was not up for discussion she was to be chaperoned by Matilda upon her uncle's orders. Sitting back in her seat of her carriage, she watched Joanna shift impatiently in her seat.

Tonight was a more special night for Joanna.

Although she has many gentleman callers there is one in particular, she wanted to see this night. She knew about her sisters dalliances which in part were improper because she is marrying Lord Ethan Humphries, Earl of Westbrook. He was broodingly handsome, but had a bad temper with his drink as some whispered. Therefore, she had her clandestine meetings while he was away.

The clock in his solar ticked incessantly. He poured another glass of whiskey and turned to stand at his window. The lit streetlights gave him an ample view of its occupants as they walked and talked. Carriages trotted here and there carrying its passengers to their destination.

A slight tap at his door demanded his answer for entry.

"Enter!" He ordered.

The familiar form of Bufford entered.

"M'lord, will you not be assisting Lady VanCamps evening affair?" Bufford questioned, looking at the clock above the fireplace.

He received the invitation weeks ago, but had no intentions of going. Such event he tried not to attend. He had to admit that at times, it was entertaining, but it grew bothersome with the downpour of idiotic chatter.

"Sorry Bufford, I am not going to attend." He answered.

Searching for words to say to Dominic, he sputtered.

"M'lord I must say it will be quite the event. Lady Amanda had asked you to attend with her." Bufford smiled with hope that finally Dominic would go to lift up his spirits.

He sat staring into the fire before him. Swirling the dark liquid in his mouth, he recalled his last encounter with Lady Amanda and her long milky thighs that snaked their way up his legs in an effort to grab his attention at The Brownford's luncheon. Her advances gained a short but seductive romp in his carriage.

She was an enticing woman eager for him. Time and circumstance would not permit such a union. She was married at the time and her husband was at the party.

He was surely going to go to hell for his rake hellish ways. His groin began to throb at the vision of her soft, plump rump in his lap and warm beneath his fingers.

The brisk clearing of Bufford's throat reminded him he waited for an answer.

"It is better I don't attend Bufford." He insisted.

"Very well M'lord, I am retiring for the night will you be in need of anything else?"

Dominic shook his head, then thought again. It was Friday after all, what was to stop him from taking a long weekend absence.

Turning, he smiled and bolted out his plan to a baffled Bufford.

"But....But...At this hour M'lord? Bufford nervously looked at the watch.

"Yes, ready some food for me, I want to leave within the hour." He ordered.

Bufford hesitated for a bit before turning on his heels to do as he was asked.

It would be a long overdue voyage for him to be finally away from the soot and smog of this city. He breathed.

Just a brief getaway for a couple of days is all he hungered for.

The ball was in full swing. The mixture of music and laughter wafted through the entrance doors. Her uncle at her side acknowledged acquaintances and friends with a smile and a nod with his nieces in tow. By the time they made it through the crowd into the main Ballroom the familiar face of Lady VanCamp came into view with an endearing smile.

"Why Emilia everyday you grow more beautiful." chimed Lady VanCamp as she painfully pinched her cheeks.

With a pretty bow, Emilia thanked her.

The overwhelming compliments poured like a bucket of water overhead. More for her than Joanna she noticed.

She bowed her head to avert the gaze from the prying, curious and smitten stares of some of the tons eligible bachelors. A languid seductive smile came from many while coy bashful bows came from the rest.

The dinner continued and they talked of many things that lasted with an informal dance to pass the night away. She watched as Joanna swayed to the music. She enjoyed the merriment sitting and watching.

She watched Joanna menacingly come her way with other girls trailing behind her that devious smile she has when she has something planned made her nervous.

"Oh sister!" She pouted, Pulling Emilia to her feet. Pulling away shyly, she saw what her sister was doing and before she could protest, she swirled her into the arms of a young man. The snickers and low claps of gloved hands excited by their work watched in awe as she gracefully fell into place with her partner's footsteps.

Miffed and embarrassed she hid her demeanor under a shy smile.

She twirled and spun all over as the onlookers admired her dancing.

"I do say milady your beauty and grace are most becoming" the young man said in a low voice.

She looked up to him.

He was very handsome with a boyish look perhaps he was about a year or two older than she was, she being 16.

"Forgive me if I have not properly introduced myself, my name is Adam VanCamp." He smiled.

Her eyes lit up with the knowledge he was family to Lady Van-Camp.

He nodded with what he figured she would ask.

"I am her nephew" he smiled, showing beautiful pearly white teeth.

"Please to meet your acquaintance." She smiled.

After a brief conversation with him, she was relieved when she walked back to her chair. Surprisingly Joanna was not there waiting for her. Curiously, she looked around and did not see her.

She went in search for her.

Groups of people swam in front of her as she searched all over for Joanna. It was not good to be left unchaperoned Matilda was in the main hall with others talking.

Frustrated, she began to worry that Joanna took off.

She whirled in her head all the places she checked, then realized Joanna could be in the garden.

Lady VanCamp had a large beautiful garden with a gazebo.

She made her way through the crowd towards the back entrance door that led to the garden.

The dark night was welcoming; she looked around, but saw no one. She inched a bit on the walkway towards the gazebo.

The soft, familiar laugh of Joanna came to the ear.

Puzzled, she walked closer to where the laughter came from.

"Oh! Stephen you naughty man." She panted.

His husky laugh came from the middle of her bosom.

She breathed heavily when his hands found their way beneath her skirts.

His hot lips trailed her neck to her ears.

How they breathed and panted with not a care in the world. Only startled disbelieving eyes watched what was unfolding before her.

As if all alone and not a care in the world they continued their tryst. They never heard the footsteps or felt the presence that they were being watched.

The vision before her was unreal. The uncompromising position her sister was in was new to her. She was never really taught the way of woman and men in intimacy, only what she overheard in gossip.

"Oh! Stephen?" Johanna moaned.

And her cheeks grew hot.

She watched with the little moonlight the astonishing view of her sister straddled in Stephen's lap. Her breasts exposed and dress pulled all the way up to her waist. A slight feeling of warmth and embarrassment crept up her cheeks as her sister shamefully let his hand disappear between her legs. Her ears burned with all the moaning and panting. Shaking her head, she could not believe what she was seeing how she was letting Stephen touch her so. Her chest ached with hurt because she detested him.

In shock, she watched as he exposed himself and laid her on the bench beneath him. Her gasps and moans began with his movement of his hips.

The passion of the two went on only to be cut short of Emilia shouting Joanna's name.

"What are you doing out here." Joanna hissed pushing Stephen off of her.

She watched Joanna lower her skirts and hide her breasts back in her bodice. Fixing herself and her composure, she walked passed Stephen that was doing the same.

Emilia's voice cracked

"I was looking for you," she whispered, lowering her head.

"Well, you found me, now go," Joanna scowled angrily.

Shaking her head Emilia refused to leave.

"No, I will not leave without you." She protested shooting Steven daggers of hate.

"I won't leave you alone with this...Monster," she blurted out.

Joanna stepped before Stephen lunged at Emilia.

"You listen here you little bitch...." He hissed.

"If you do not leave with me this instant Joanna I will tell Uncle of what I saw," she threatened with little courage she could muster up to make it believable.

Joanna rift with anger yanked Emilia by her arm with so much force a scream came from her.

"You're hurting Me." She cried.

"It will be much worse if you open your mouth." Joanna warned.

"What you're doing is wrong Joanna! You're making a big mistake," she pleaded.

The heated voice of Stephen piped into their argument.

"A mistake that will cost you, dearly if you open your bloody mouth." He clenched his jaw.

"You bastard, all you do is accost and grope me," she whispered with disgust.

"And then your filthy hands caress and feel my sister!" She cried out.

Joanna watched as Stephen pushed passed her and grabbed Emilia by the shoulders and throat, then shook her.

"You don't know how much I pray for the day to get you alone," he breathed near her lips.

"And you don't know how much I pray for the day you return under the rock you came from." She yelled.

He began to pull her. However, Joanna stopped him and yanked her from his grip before he could do her any harm.

"I will handle her." Joanna said over her shoulders, pulling Emilia behind her.

With that said, Johanna dragged her across the lawn towards the front side of the house. She hushed Emilia, while she pulled her through a winding back street familiar as a shorter way home.

Emilia begged her to stop. The whole time Joanna spewed curses at her. She has never seen her so angry.

The dark alley way led to the beginning of another road. When they got to the end, a carriage rolled in at breakneck speed and halted before them.

It was Stephen.

He ordered them to get in. Her heart slammed in her chest that something was not right.

Joanna opened the carriage door, pulled it open and yanked Emilia to get in. Slipping from her grip, she ran.

She barely got far before a hard arm encircled her waist so hard she could barely breathe. Stephens's large hands covered her mouth to muffle her screams.

With little effort, she was tossed on the floor of the carriage before Joanna.

With her hair in a mess toppled about her face, she trembled at the hand that grabbed for her. With a cry, she slapped it away and threw herself on the opposite chair. Out of breath, she faced her sister.

"Why are you doing this Joanna?" She cried out.

"I cannot risk you ruining this for me, Emilia." Joanna plumped beside her and grabbed her arm digging her nails deep.

"Ruin what, your chance to become his whore?" Emilia said icily.

The sting of Joanna's hand across her face startled her. Holding her cheek, she shot a hurt look of disbelief at Joanna.

Frightened, she sat back into the corner of the chair. The murderous glare that set in Joanna's eye made her recoil further.

Tear filled eyes followed by her words.

"I cannot be married to Ethan, I do not love him." She shook her head.

All knew that the earl had a penchant for the drink and a heavy hand when angered. It set fear in Joanna's heart, fear that pushed her to do the unthinkable.

Within seconds, she grabbed Emilia and they began to struggle with so much force. Johanna slammed her against the carriage door, throwing it open, Emilia screamed.

"Joanna, what are you doing?" The speed of the carriage was very fast.

Holding on to Joanna's skirt, Emilia screamed and begged. Joanna picked and pulled at her fingers clawing at her dress trying to avoid being pulled out as well.

The look of fright in Emilia's eyes along with tears stared into Joanna's.

"Forgive me sister." Joanna cried, closing her eyes and looking away for a brief second before she finally pulled Emilia's fingers free.

The final scream of her name from Emilia's lips disappeared into the dark night.

With a screeching halt the carriage stopped, thrashing her about. The opposite door swung open. Stephen's look of fright looked up to Joanna's tear streaked face.

"Bloody hell! What did you do, Joanna?" Panicked, his voice shrieked.

Staring at him, little emotion and shock came in her voice.

"I pushed her out," she cried.

With a ring of curses he ran back to look for Emilia. The loud crash of the water drew him to realize he was near the docks. Boats lined up and bounced violently in the water. He frantically searched for her.

The lump in the road further down got him into a panic, running towards her he slid to his knees beside her limp body.

It was contorted and mangled, she lay lifeless. Fear gripped at his heart of the worst.

The whimper behind him came into view.

"Is she alive?" Regret and agony was in her cries.

Looking up at her with hate and disdain, he warned her.

"You better hope she still lives. Why did you do this?"

She did not answer, only cried.

He leaned his head forward and placed it by her lips. Her breathing was faint.

Closing his eyes, he had no idea what to do. He could not take her home like this.

The idea struck him, he looked at the nearby boats. He needed to get her in it. For sure she would be found in the morning by then they will be long gone.

Quickly he gathered her in his arms. Joanna sniffled.

"What are you going to do?"

"We cannot leave her here in the road; I must put her in the boat."
He said harshly.

Her featherweight bared no burden for him to move quickly. He
gently placed among the ropes of the anchor.

Cursing himself, he removed her slippers, gown and the rest of her
clothing. It would be hard to identify her if she did not have on those
clothes. No one would know who she is if she lives, until her uncle
calls a search.

Tossing her belongings into the water, he jumped to the dock. The
snicker and hoof steps of an oncoming carriage, picked up their pace
to leave. Within seconds, they were out of sight before the other
carriage pulled up.

Chapter 3

Jolting to a stop, he leaned forward and pushed open the door. Hopping out, Bufford met Dominic on the side of the carriage and helped him unload his baggage. With few words exchanged in the task, Bufford turned to look at him.

"Now remember, I will be gone for a week or two. I will be on the Grisham Estates attending to the lands and what needs to be done there.

With a nod, Bufford agreed.

Understanding fully well he must attend to what his father left for him. He turned to step off the dock onto the boat. Within minutes of prepping and loading everything on, he set sail and began to pull away from the dock, away from the ton and away from everything.

The dark night engulfed him and the boat in the water. He breathed the fresh air. Looking up at the stars he stretched out and relaxed, enjoying the soft waves. It was a perfect clear night. Staring into the dark glittery, starry night, he drifted off to sleep.

Some time had passed and Emilia finally fought her way out of the darkness she was drowning in. The silence terrified her; she heard nothing and felt chilled. Slowly she opened her eyes and gasped for air. She felt the unbearable pain that jolted through her, a low whimper escaped her. Unable to move her left arm, she moved her right with so much pain. She felt for her surroundings. Her heart stopped when she passed her hand over her bare skin, she was naked. Slight feeling was returning back to her now aching body that it brought a sharp cry when she tried to move and couldn't. Frantically, she cried the pain was excruciating.

Her raspy voice barely audible began to cry out for help.

The soft cry beckoned for help. Slowly he drifted in and out of sleep, but the cry came again and his lids heavily opened. Silently, he listened again.

Was his mind playing with him?

Was he dreaming?

Sitting up, eyes wide open he frowned.

The cry came again from the rear of the boat.

He stood quickly grabbed his lantern and walked towards the sound. He neared the rear of the boat, shining the lantern in the darkness. The soft glow of light revealed a naked young girl weeping.

With a curse, he quickly lowered the lamp and pulled off his shirt to cover her.

"My god, what happened to you?" He whispered nervously.

He quickly knelt beside her to pick her up, but her anguished blood curdling scream just as fast stopped him. Something was wrong.

"What is wrong?" He asked in a breathless panic.

Her meek voice through sobs cried the pain was coming from her shoulder and her ankles.

He thought quickly, he would have to risk moving her below. He could not leave her like this.

"I must get you below, this is going to hurt very much," he explained.

Gentle he could no more be to avoid her scream, but it was inevitable. She ground her face into his chest and cried with the most heart wrenching scream.He only made it half way thru the doorway to the cabin before she went limp in his arms. Gently he placed her on the bed.

He lit the two wall sconces that lit the cabin up enough to see her.

He sat on the side of the bed and moved her hair away from her face. She was passed out. He felt her cheeks and was relieved of no sign of fever.

Sitting at her side, thoughts passed in his mind of how she ended up on his boat. Who was she? Where was she from? Answers at this moment he was not going to get from her. He wondered when she would awaken.

His mind swam with what to do; He was too far out to return. Set with a decision he set course for his estate.

He looked at her before going above to get the boat moving. She needed help.

The lands around the estate greeted him head on as he carefully walked with the young girl in his arms. The manor, although solitary was big and opulent. He walked the cobblestone pathway to the entrance door. With a nudge, he managed to get it open. Entering, he looked around to the empty waiting area.

"Hello! Is anyone here?" He called out

Although the manor has been unoccupied for years, Helmsley an elderly groundskeeper stayed in the manor. The soft baritone voice of a man came from the stairs above.

"M'lord, you have returned so soon, " he came quickly.

The old man met him with surprise. His pallor began to whiten when he looked at the young girl limp in his arms. Startled eyes shot up to look at an annoyed look in Dominic's eyes. Nervously, he overlooked the petite form and noticed that she was not dressed, but in a thin large shirt.

Annoyed Dominic breathed. Clenching his jaw, he shot the old man an impatient stare.

"Aye, she is still alive if that is what you are wondering," he hissed.

Leaving Helmsley to fall into step behind him, he marched up the stairs two at a time to his quarters he stays in when he is there.

The not so welcoming cool decorated room was as he left it. Helmsley quickly walked over to the large windows and drew the heavy curtains back to let in the bright morning light.

Placing her on the large bed, he drew back to let the light fall on her to see her clearly. The gasp that came from Helmsley beat him to it.

"She is but a young girl, m'lord. What happened to her?" He searched Dominic's face for answers.

Arms crossed before his chest, he shook his head.

"I don't know. I found her on my boat."

He sat at her side of the bed and softly pulled the shirt over her shoulder to examine her. The gasp of Helmsley caught his ear and he knew it was bad. Her shoulder looked discolored, swollen and no doubt dislocated. Miffed and bothered he knew nothing about this or how to fix it. He shot Helmsley a sad look.

"She is injured Helmsley, she needs to be seen by a physician." He turned to continue checking for more bruises and noticed her ankles were slightly discolored as well.

"M'lord, but there is no one." He gave Dominic a frightened look.

"Well you bloody well better find someone old man, and fast." He stood, walking to Helmsley.

The poor old man backed away from Dominic icy glare of rage and walked out leaving him alone.

He stood and watched the young girl. Her long hair lay askew, her cherubic face peaceful with long lashes, pert nose and pretty lips. His mind toyed with question after question but had no answers. Time had passed and he impatiently waited for the physician. Suddenly the boisterous voices came from the stairway. Helmsley entered the room with the physician.

Entering Helmsley shyly pointed towards the bed. The physician's frightful gaze looked at the girl and gasped, clutching his leather bag to his chest.

"Dear God, What happened to this poor child?"

Annoyance boiled at Dominic resolve.

"That is why we summoned you, to find out what is wrong and to see if you can see to her injuries."

The physician neared the side of the bed and placed his hand above her forehead and throat.

"She has no fever, which is good."

Resting his bag on the bed, he continued to examine her.

Helmsley nervously stood beside Dominic watching the physician do his work.

After a long examination, he stood and turned to Dominic.

"What is wrong with her?" He asked.

Weary eyes saddened. "She has a separated shoulder and fractured ankles on both feet."

"What must be done?" He asked.

"We must reset the bone, M'lord that is the only way to fix her shoulder and then we bandage her ankles."

"Well, let us get on with it before she awakens," he ordered.

Upon the physician's instructions he followed what was to be done. Getting into position the doctor paused and looked at Dominic.

"M'lord would you like for me to put her under." The physician asked.

The puzzling question made Dominic frown.

"What do you mean?"

Clearing his throat the physician cracked a nervous smile.

"Forgive me m'lord, but I have never set a bone before...Well, not at least in a person...A human...Err, only in animals..... Mainly horses."

"What say you, are you not a physician?" Dominic incredulous glare shot right from him to Helmsley.

"No, my lord, I'm a Veterinarian. I tend to the local farm animals." The poor man inched back a bit as Dominic's look of disbelief turned deadly.

"Why the hell did you bring an animal doctor, does she look like a horse to you, Helmsley?" He hissed in anger.

"Forgive me m'lord, he was all I could find in such short notice." Helmsley wiped his brow of sweat and nervously looked at them both.

Brushing off Helmsley, he ordered the physician to continue. He had no time to waste.

"Are you sure m'lord you do not want me to administer..." the warning glare from Dominic immediately stopped him.

"Not unless you want a quick death old man, lets get on with this. My patience is waning thin." He gnarled.

They got into position both men on each side of her, he watched as the physician placed his hand over her shoulder and extended her arm. Bearing down and holding her in place, the man yanked her arm until a pop and crack resonated from her shoulder.

Thankful she was not awake for this, he laid her gently against the pillows.

After making a makeshift sling out of cloth and her feet were bandaged the physicians gave ointment for her shoulder and laudanum for the pain.

"Do you know how she could have sustained injuries such as this?" He questioned.

With a frown, he folded the leather bag shut and stood before him.

"I can only think of one way M'lord, she could have jumped from a horse or carriage, but, there is no way to be entirely sure how this happened until she awakens." He sadly looked at her.

"How long would it take for her to be completely healed and recover?"

"Depending on how fast she heals can take weeks; she will need much rest and must not be moved until then." The physician eyed the poor girl.

"I would appreciate your absolute discretion on this matter and what has occurred here today is repeated to no one." Dominic warned.

With a curt nod in response that he understood, the physician took his leave.

He walked over to the bed and sat at her side. She barely moved when they reset her shoulder. There was little he could do for her now, but watch over her.

Chapter 4

The morning light danced on her closed eyelids. As if breathing for the first time she inhaled deeply. Slowly, her eyes heavy with sleep opened. Groggy and weak she looked at her surroundings. Blinking and trying to clear her foggy mind, confusion set on her instantly.

Grimacing with pain she pulled herself up into a sitting position and leaned against the pillows. Her arm was wrapped in a sling, her feet were bandaged and propped on pillows. Looking around, she wondered where she was. The massive poster bed sat adjacent a large beautiful window with elegant drapes and tassels, the room furnished in opulent grandeur, was fitted for someone of wealth. She looked down at herself and gasped. She wore nothing but a thin shirt that covered very little of her.

Not able to move much with her right hand, she reached for the coverlet and covered herself. Her hand went up and touched her hair, the massive mess above her head was evident from the feel of loose locks. Smoothing away her loose strands and removing the remaining pins she combed her finger through it. Silky waves of brown fell past her shoulder down to her sides. Pulling the sheets to her lap, she played with the strange images in her mind wondering where she was. And who brought her here? Lost in her thought she did not notice the tall figure that stood by the door until he spoke.

"Good Morning, I see someone has finally awoken." Dominic stood with crossed arms against the open door jam.

His smile was sensual and soft.

He had walked in to find her removing the pins from her hair. He silently observed her. She protectively sank further into the pillows and pulled the sheets closer to her chin. Shyly she looked down with her hand in her lap.

He walked closer to lean against the bedpost closely observing her. After a while he looked at her shoulder.

"Does it still pain you?" She followed his gaze to the sling on her arm. Shaking her head, she looked at it. "Only with slight movement," Her soft meek voice assured him.

For a brief moment, they fell silent. He cleared his throat and stepped forward to sit at her bedside. "Forgive me for my rudeness; my name is Dominic McAllister, Marquess of Grisham."

Demurely she gave a shy smile. "Please to meet your acquaintance M'lord, I am Emilia Westham"

A small grin tugged at the side of his mouth, he noticed long lashes fanned her cheeks while she looked down. He looked her over and noticed the silky long brown hair that rested in soft curls on her shoulder and fell to her elbow. It was long and beautiful. She had the look of a well-groomed young girl of status.

"Can you tell me Emilia, What happened to you?" His soft baritone voice hypnotically pulled her eyes to look at his face.

She sat silent for a while trying to remember.

She looked up at him.

The very few men she has actually encountered and interacted with looked nothing like him.

His eyes were as blue as sapphire gems, hair black as midnight, the shadow of a beard gave him a breathtaking look. With her thoughts lodged in her mind, she searched for the answer she was looking for.

"I am afraid not, M'lord, all I can remember is being at a dinner party."

His puzzled look waited for her to continue.

Silently staring into the distance with a frown, she briefly closed her eyes and began to rub her forehead trying to remember.

"I remember being at Lady VanCamps dinner party. From there everything went dark and... I remembered you covering me, " she shyly hugged herself.

His lips curled into a smile. After a while, the smile faded from his lips.

"Well under the circumstances due to your injuries you cannot get out of bed for a couple of days."

He watched her eyes widen in disbelief.

"A couple of days?" She asked.

"Weeks even," He added.

He watched her face go from disbelief to terrified.

"Weeks!" She was horrified.

"A few months at the least" The humorous tone to his voice made her look at him.

He had the laugh in his eyes at her bewildered stare when it turned into a teasing smile.

"You're wicked m'lord." She smiled, her eyes danced with his humorous joking.

He chuckled.

After a brief exchange of words, he repeated what the physician had told him.

"But, in truth our real dilemma is there is no one to attend to you." He pointed out the obvious.

"Oh my, that is a dilemma!" She lowered her eyes.

He looked at her, his expression softened.

"I sent word with Helmsley to find someone to assist you. But, I fear it will be some time before they return." He assured her.

With an optimistic air to her reply, he chuckled.

"I guess due to circumstances there is really nothing we can do. Although it is improper, it is inevitable that we are alone. I believe we can manage until then. Don't you think M'lord?"

With a chuckle, he agreed. "Yes, indeed."

And, yes indeed they did. Every day he found himself perched on the edge of her bed. They talked and laughed over gossip they heard and people they both knew. Their conversations day by day had a pleasant air to it.

They focused on a relaxing card game after their mid-morning meal.

"And your opinion of Lady Hilde?" He peaked over his cards.

Lowering her cards she rolled her eyes to the side trying to think. He sat crossed leg facing her.

"Too pompous for her own good." She wrinkled her nose.

Dominic looked up to her with a quizzical stare.

"Is she not the one that they say is quite daft?" Studying his cards, he threw one down.

Emilia looked at him struggling to contain her laughter.

"Of course, she had poor Mumsy taxidermed,"

With a frown, he looked at her not understanding her

"Who is Mumsy?" he frowned.

With a cool glare she looked at him, fighting to maintain her composure.

"The bedraggled white ball of fur she carries everywhere, is Mumsy"

He stared at her still confused.

" .....Her dead poodle." she added.

He stared at Emilia for a brief moment and collapsed in a sputtering heap of laughter that his shoulders shook and she followed immediately.

The day was never dull in her presence, he marveled.

She was fascinated with his stories of sailing. He observed that underneath all her beauty she was also very smart. She grew more interested in understanding his views of the world.

Dominic, as the days passed by he grew fond of her and anticipated her presence everyday as she did his.

~.~.~.~.~..~She sat before frustrated before the mirror. It was evidently very hard to brush her hair with one hand. Her shoulder was beginning to throb. In defeat she let out a puff of pent up air and placed her brush on the table.

"Need some help?" Dominic asked.

She looked up into the mirror at his reflection there eyes met. He stood leaning against the door frame watching her.

She glanced down at her brush picking it up she turned to face him and held it up in her hand.Silently she waited and looked at him. Her heart fluttered as she watched his lips curl into a smile then a gorgeous grin.He pushed away from the door and walked slowly towards her gently taking the brush from her hand, she turned and watched him through the mirror as he softly place the bristles to the crown of her head and stroked downward.

It was a heavenly feeling she got lost in and she enjoyed it. It was a daily morning routine he happily fell into as well.

She giggled innocently at his attempts to help her comb her hair.

"I don't understand why, if I can make a sailors knot, I can't make a damnable braid" he fussed with the long brown mane of curls before him.

A quick sigh turned into a soft laugh followed by her giggle as she fought to gain control of the hairbrush.

The daily routine of taking care of her slowly fell into a normal flow they grew accustomed to. By the weeks end, the awkwardness of taking her bath changed when he decided to try to help her but blindfolded.

They played chess and enjoyed reading stories in books from his massive collection in his library. Ever so often, he carried her to his study where they lay on the floor by the fire stretched out like children laughing. He had never felt this much freedom before and neither has she. Helmsley would see the two and would smile at how they were together.

Chapter 5

The dreary morning promised heavy rain.

Stretched out in bed with their bodies laying in opposite corners and their heads touching, they listened to the light pitter-patter of rain. The gloomy day brought a sense of tranquility with them both.

"Well, what shall we do today, a game of chess, read a bit or game of cards???" Dominic chimed..

He waited for her answer.

With an unsure tone in her voice that sound more of a wish than a decision she breathed.

"Let's play in the rain." She shrugged.

Nervously she waited for him to chuckle at her request and deny such a silly thought. But her heart lurched in disbelief when he agreed.

"Ok, let us play in the rain!"

He sat up jubilee and pulled her along with him. Her giggle and laugh bounced off the room walls. He turned for her to jump on his back. Careful not to touch her ankles, he told her to hold on. She caressed his shoulder and hugged tight.

Helmsley came to them thru the hall as they neared the last step on the stairway. He looked up at the two. A bit surprised he smiled coyly at the two, understanding that since Emilia could not walk he had to carry her down. She was absolutely lovely her hair loose and wavy bounced with every movement.

"M'lord would you or Lady Emilia care for some tea or something to eat." Helmsley smiled at him watching Dominic turned an asking glance at Emilia over his shoulder, with a twitch of her nose she giggled and shook her head.

"No thank you, Helmsley" He chuckled with laughter in his eyes.

He stood in awe about the strange news they were going to play in the rain.

"But, but m'lord it's pouring out there and you both can catch a deathly cold in all of it."

A bit miffed at their childish mocking faces. He gave in to their crazed idea and watched them walk out the door.

"Oh! Helmsley keep dry towels for us and the fire burning in my study" he ordered.

"Yes, M'lord. " He smiled with a nod and waved to a giddy Emilia.

The husky laugh and shriek were signs that the rain was chilly. He walked slowly across the lawn with her on his back. He slowly lowered her to the wet grass and sat beside her.

He looked over to her, her eyes closed and she tipped her head back stretching out her arms. As if lying in water afloat, she let the cool rain pour over her. He lost himself watching her. She had a beauty and spirit about her that warmed his heart. What sat next to him was an exquisite and charming creature. The smile on her lips wet with rain revealed pearly white teeth as she smiled. She lowered her arms content in her feelings.

Her eyes opened slowly and looked up at him. Her heart quickened to see him looking down at her. They silently stared into each other's eyes. She shyly looked away while her teeth tugged at her bottom lip nervously. A soft grin grew on his lips when he saw her cheeks turning a slight pink.

The soft shiver she released was indication they were in the rain for too long.

They both agreed it was time to go in. He bent and swiftly picked her up and carried her.

The warmth in his study gave them a cozy feeling.

"I believe if we stay any longer in the rain we would shrivel like raisins." He mentioned.

All dried off and sitting before the fire, he placed a blanket around her shoulders.

The heavy rain continued. They sat on the floor and concentrated on a good old game of Piquet. Well into the game, he stood and walked over to a nearby table and poured himself some Whiskey. Her curious eyes peeked over her cards and followed him.

He turned and took a swallow.

"Milord, why do I get tea and you get wine?" She asked, puzzled her eye drew together into a frown.

His eyes lit with a grin at her innocent question. He looked into the cup and shook his head with a laugh.

"This is not wine." He lifted it for her to see.

Her face frowned again and gave a most curious look that made him chuckle.

"This...My little friend is the devils drink." He teased.

Still, her eyes regarded him with a puzzled look.

"Why can I not have some?" She continued to frown.

With a side-glance in a teasing way, he wagged his finger.

"No, this drink is not for you. It is too strong."

"How strong?" She asked more curiously.

He eyed her for a while, taking in her unwavering expectant glare to share that mysterious drink.

What would it hurt if she tried a little? He thought to himself.

She kept looking at him while he pondered his decision. He doubted she would like it. With a roguish grin, he turned and poured a little in a smaller glass.

"Very well...You are warned."

He walked and sat facing her.

Her eyes smiling, reached for the amber liquid in the glass.

Emerald pools lit up with excitement. Unsure, she hesitated and lifted it to her lips. She stopped to look at Dominic. His teasing gaze and grin made her giggle. His reassuring nod when he raised his cup to his lips was all she needed.

The amber liquid turned warm in her mouth as she sipped very little at first. The firey burn that traveled down her throat made her wince. Determined to prove him wrong, she continued until it was all gone.

She looked at him and smiled, showing him the empty glass.

"It has a peculiar taste." She scrunched her nose up and giggled.

With raised eyebrows, he let out a boisterous laugh.

"Does it now?" His eyes twinkled with laughter.

"May I have more?" She held up her glass with a beseeching look.

He leaned back and watched her. He couldn't say no, he honestly wanted to see what a little whiskey would do to her. Besides, he had no one to drink with but her. He agreed, then stood up and brought the whole bottle.

"Now little miss I present to you, one of many drinks that has been the downfall of many men by dampening their wits during gambling." He eyed the liquid while pouring it and handing it to her.

She shook her head softly and rolled her eyes mockingly

"You're funny." She giggled.

The feel of the whiskey was beginning to take its effect on her after she finished her third glass. They laughed and continued playing Piquet. He began to watch her even in her present state she was smiling. After a while of not being able to concentrate on the game and making so many mistakes, it was evident she was drunk.

She eyed the last few ounces of whiskey in the bottle. He grinned and shook his head that it was enough. She inched closer to him.

"Just a little bit more." She crawled closer to him swaying.

Dominic was in awe at the way the flickering light from the flames danced upon her skin. She met his eyes and he found he couldn't look away.

"You my friend are well into your cups." He gently smoothed back a strand of hair from her face.

She sat before him and looked into his eyes. He caressed her cheek. He was lost in her stare, his eyes lowered to look at her lips. They were so delectable and needed to be kissed. His groin throbbed with just the thought of kissing her. He needed to fight this sudden urge to run his fingers thru her hair and lay her on the ground to caress her body and make love to her. His heart pummeled in his chest when she looked away from his seductive stare and began picking up the cards, but he could not do it. To kiss her like this, in this state would be utterly wrong.

She broke his concentration by turning around to lay her head on his lap. With her hair fanned out draped above his legs. She was clueless as to what she was making him feel.

Her eyes danced as they looked up at him. Holding the stack of cards in one hand , Her other hand reached out and softly touched his cheek.

"M'lord, why are you not married?" So pleasant her voice was that his smile made her grin.

"Because, beautiful, I am damaged goods not eligible for the marriage market." His voice was low and husky.

Her eyes furrowed confused. She sat up to look at him. Long hair fanned around her cherubic face, she was mesmerizing.

"M'lord, how are you damaged?" Her look changed and she looked so adorable, her green eyes held such a concerned look.

He lifted one knee and placed his arm on it. He idly began to twirl a long soft curl in his hand. He concentrated on the color, texture and silky feel of it. He looked down at her.

"I am considered the rake-hell of the ton, a womanizer, a gambler, and a libertine." He grinned at the numerous names dealt him due to his endeavors.

His seductive look mesmerized her.

Her innocent glare searched his face.

" Is any of that true, m'lord?"

He chuckled and looked over her face and caressed it.

"Yes, beautiful... Let's just say that I cannot be trusted with the pretty lasses."

She lowered her gaze for a while, then sadly looked up at him.

"I trust you, I don't believe any of those things about you," Her eyes sparkled with her opinion.

He sighed softly. "You are too innocent to see me for what I trully am."

With a determined glare she held his.

"I am 16 soon to be 17, m'lord I am not a child," She lowered her gaze.

"Besides, all those things m'lord, if they were true, then I would not be safe here with you," She pointed out.

She had no idea how wrong she was. Her innocence blinded her of the hungry feeling he felt for her. His sheer will to take her to his bed was a barrier he held up for his dear life.

He chuckled at her innocent observation.

"How would it look to the ton if I ravished a defenseless beautiful injured girl, I would surely be hanged" His eyes held hers.

Her sullen look at not being ravished because she was injured, was an all-new high for him. With a boisterous laugh, he pulled her close to embrace her.

He laid her beside him and propped himself on his elbow to look down at her.

His gaze upon her turned serious and meaningful.

"I would never do anything to hurt you or ruin your reputation. I may be a rake, but I am not a lout, Do you understand?" His voice held a soft tone.

Her heart pattered with his soft stare.

With a quick nod of her head, He noticed her gaze slowly getting sleepy. No doubt, the Whiskey really took a toll on her. He was surprised she held up so well.

"Dominic?" Her voice sleepily whispered, his name.

For some odd reason his name on her lips sent an emotional wave over him. He looked at her. Her eyes opened slowly and held his. The beautiful green gems in her eyes held such a look that it stiffened him. Her delicate fingers rose and brushed his face. The way she did it warmed his heart and sent a ripple through his body. He gently held them to his cheek and lightly kissed the inside of her palm. Such a gesture quickened her heart.

His gaze returned to hers.

"If I had to be ravished, I would only want to be ravished by you," She whispered sweetly.

The words that came from her lips left him in complete shock and awe; her Whiskey induced words were so honest. Primal instincts set in that he could not control. Guided by her fingers, he lowered his head, her eyes held his with a look of wanting. His lips brushed hers. Her lips soft and sweet returned the kiss. Such a soft sigh escaped her breath. He lifted his head to look down at her. He called her name. Her head fell to the side and cuddled into his arm. She fell asleep.

He lay staring into her sleeping face. She was breathtaking. He developed such a feeling for her that it formed a lump in his throat. Nevertheless, as he said, he was not an eligible marriage prospect. His reputation would sully hers. No doubt when they return there would be no telling what would be said about their unchaperoned stay here.

With a brief sigh, he smiled to himself. On the good side, she would not remember any of this in the morning.

He picked her up, cradled her in his arms and took her to her room. The warm, welcoming fire slowly danced in the fireplace. He placed her on the bed and pulled her covers up. He gently brushed a kiss on her cheek and looked her over then turned to leave.

Chapter 6

Morning came with a welcoming light. As usual, he awoke bright and early he got dressed. Eager to see his beautiful friend, he donned his boots and walked out of his room. He walked across the hall and met Helmsley coming towards him with a tray of breakfast.

"Good morning, Helmsley " he beamed.

"Good Morning to you, M'lord." He smiled back.

Eyeing the tray before him Helmsley pointed out the delicious contents of toast, strawberry preserves, fruits and a strong cup of coffee.

He eyed the old man with an arched brow who returned the silent glare with a calm look as he knew she would need it. The grin that pulled at Helmesly's lips made Dominic laugh.

"She will definitely be needing this." He eyed the black coffee in the cup and picked it candidly off the tray.

With an agreeing nod, he followed Dominic after a slight tap at the door. Slightly poking his head thru the door the room was quiet.

Slowly they entered with a gesture to be quiet Helmsley quickly placed the tray on the nearby table before the window. Drawing the curtains, he let in the splendid morning sunlight that illuminated the room. With a quick nod, he left them alone.

He placed the hot cup of coffee on the nightstand and sat at her side, leaning across her he looked down at her.

His playful baritone voice stirred her. "Emilia, wake up."

With a moan, she turned her face away from the light and burrowed deeper into the sheets.

"We will have none of that Miss." He chuckled, pulling the covers away from her face.

With another moan, she turned to open one eye slowly. Stirring more she turned and shook her head not wanting to get up.

"I must look the way I feel m'lord, don't look at me." She mumbled softly into her pillow.

He laughed, shaking his head.

"How do you feel?" He leaned closer and brushed all her hair from her face.

"I feel as if I were thrown on top of a boat." Her mocking grin turned into a throaty giggle when he caught on to her joke.

He let out a hearty laugh.

Calming down from the cackle of laughter that lit up their morning he sighed, shaking his head in awe at her humor.

"Minx." He sighed.

She wrinkled her nose with a grin that melted his heart. She was simply adorable.

With deep breaths, they looked at each other. Quickly he leaned over to the table and carefully placed in her hands the hot cup of coffee.

"I do believe young lady, that you are in need of this."

She gladly took the warm brew within her hands and breathed in the aroma that woke her senses and sent a wash of warmth over her body.

Meanwhile, she sipped Dominic stood and sat at the foot of her bed and began to examine her bandaged ankles.

He unwrapped the long white cloth and observed that the swelling went down a bit.

She watched as he lowered his head and concentrated on each one. Her heart began to race at the touch of his strong warm hands caressing her ankle and soles of her feet.

"There appears to be no more swelling," he said.

Gently he massaged and rubbed it, moving his thumbs over the tender spot of her ankle. He was torturing her senses and she was slowly melting with it. Calming the odd sensation she was feeling it brought a strange sense of awareness, she gently closed her eyes and looked away.

Breaking her thoughts away, he continued talking to her unaware of the hungry glare staring at him. He was gorgeous in every way. She licked her lips and pretended to pay attention to his questions.

"Does this hurt?" He looked up into her eyes.

"No." She said coolly hiding the quiver in her tone.

He continued until he was done.

With a frown, she could not see in his eyes, he hid it from his voice.

"In no time we will be able to return home." He looked up.

Her eyes turned sad, and sulky.

Not understanding what he said wrong. He watched her lower her gaze and hide her face.

Concerned, he crossed over and plopped to the pillow beside her.

Sitting up against the headboard beside her he leaned closer to her, tilted her chin up and looked down into her face.

"What is wrong?"

Lowering her gaze, she turned her face away.

He sat silently at her side. She broke the silence and told him of her unhappy existing life she lives in the care of her uncle. Although he was not cruel, he was indeed too rigid and uncaring. Her aunt Margaux, barely speaks to her because of the busy life of her tea parties and luncheons and other womanly affairs she attends. Her sister that was distant in body and soul because she did not live with her and when she visited they barely spoke. And, Stephen the vile scoundrel that at every chance he could, he would accost her and make inappropriate advances towards her.

His blood boiled at the story. It was incredulous to think she could live like that.

Head bent her eyes stared at her lap, she breathed words that his ears did not want to hear.

"It is what I am destined to live and it shall be so, until I am married."

She dashed away a tear.

He sat and fumed over the whole ordeal. She was young and vibrant with life and she lived amongst the very people that in the snap of a finger will draw the very life from her. He didn't want to return with her either. If he could, he would stay with her here away from all that did her harm. Her delicate nature undid his resolve to never marry.

But, that was not up for debate, he would not be able to bare her such a blow to be married to him. They would be the gossip and talk of the ton, she so desperately ran from. He gambled, drank and did immoral things with the ladies, Married women. Although it would be very shocking for most to see the delicate wallflower in the company of such a scoundrel as he. The scandal..Oh! The scandal!

Chapter 7

She sat quietly at the edge of the bed. She flexed her foot just enough to loosen the stiffness of her ankle. She hesitated, and then slowly stood up.

Taking a few steps forward, she winced at the pain.

The cool swoosh of the door opened and with a blink of an eye before she lost her balance and slid to the floor, he was there beside her, holding her.

With her face buried in his shirt, she cried out. Her ankles began to throb.

"I fear this indicates you are not fully healed." He lifted her up and placed her back in bed.

He looked at her face the clear expression of pain creased her brow.

"Do want something for the pain?" He asked. Watching her immediately nod her head and dashing away a tear.

Immediately he stood and went for some warm tea.

Leaning back against the pillows, she closed her eyes.

The sleeping draught put in her tea dimmed her senses a bit. Drowsily she watched Dominic crawl to the opposite side of her. His voice began to fade. The warmth of his hand caressed her cheek. The scent of him, comforted her. She drifted off into a peaceful sleep her pain, but a memory.

The days passed by and recovery became more and more irritating for her. She detested not being able to move around freely.

She felt trapped, no different from what she felt at home. Angrily, she sat and looked at the bandages at her ankles. Miffed that she couldn't remember what happened. Did she jump from somewhere? Why were her clothes removed? She felt upset she was in this predicament.

He watched her from the door. Her mind was elsewhere.

Her mood he can tell was not a good one. Her eyes misted with unshed tears, just kept that blank stare. He watched as her hands flexed and unflexed into fists recalling her thoughts. Whatever it is, he needed to put her mind at ease.

With a brief tap, he entered.

Immediately he caught her attention and her mood changed. Her eyes lit up and held his gaze.

"We look very pensive today."

He watched her dash away a tear.

They grew silent.

"Do you miss your family, Emilia?" He looked at her with concerned eyes.

Lowering her head, she had no clue how to answer that question. She battled for an answer she could not find.

"The question m'lord is if they miss me?" She gently shrugged her reply.

His eyes saddened. How can someone not miss her? It was inconceivable to think they would not.

He tried to change up their mood.

"What exciting thing shall we do now?"

Her eyes widened with an idea. With an asking stare, she begged.

"Can we go riding?"

His eyebrow raised and he thought for a while.

"I don't see why not, it sounds like a great idea," He agreed.

With a smile, he carried her down to the stables. He sat her down on a large pile of hay as she watched him saddle and ready a horse.

She sat back and watched in awe how he easily prepared the large horse for their ride. Her focus was on the tight way how his trousers fit his muscular legs. His impressive shoulders moved beneath his white linen shirt, rolled up with the sleeves at his elbows. Her attention remained riveted on him until he turned and she quickly averted her gaze.

Her featherweight posed no difficulty for him as he sat her sideways above the horse.

He quickly mounted and secured her close to him before going off into a slow trot.

They rode the large countryside lost in the marvels of its vast beauty. Lush green expanded everywhere. She lay back against him as they slowly rode through the open land. He pointed out ducks and their ducklings walking and the animals that scurried off with their approach. The day was beautiful. Her nearness only quickened his heart, her laughter even more. When she leaned back against him, he closed his eyes because she just felt so good against him. Her hair was so soft the breeze that built up and blew on them whisked the sweet scent of Vanilla and Lavendar to his nose. A smile tugged at his lips, remembering Helmsley telling him that it goes in their water as he questioned his action with the liquid from a vile poured in her bath.

"Or do you prefer she smell like a musty old goat m'lord." he smiled. The duddy old man knew more than what he led on. Nevertheless, he was thankful for the help.

His hold on her made her feel all sorts of things.

How was she going to explain her time here with no chaperone? She could only imagine the look of sheer shock on her aunt's face at her explaining how she took her baths with a blindfolded Dominic. The thought only made heat creep up her cheeks. It felt awkward and forbidden, but at the same time good. She smiled at how he would sit with his back towards her blindfolded, threatening that he would take it off if she did not hurry and stop flicking water at him. All of this would surely make her aunt swoon at the thought.

Shortly after some time, her ankles healed and he slowly helped her around to regain her strength. Their days continued all the same, but with more to do. She was smart yet innocent and quiet yet very mischievous, he smiled. There was an air about her that was very different. She caught the heart of Helmsley for sure.

He stood by the window in his study and watched her walking towards the stables. To his amazement and shock, she climbed above the horse and rode astride with no saddle. The sight of her riding the horse in such a fashion made his hairs stand on end and his thoughts immediately went to something sinful. The Gray as he called the horse pranced softly beneath his rider. She was barefoot, her skirt was pulled dangerously high enough to expose shapely, beautiful legs that hugged the Grays back, and he felt his manhood thicken. Her carefree nature piqued his interest and now that she could walk around, there was so much about her he began to see clearly how special she was.

Morning came and the commotion below stirred him in his sleep, the shrill scream toppled him off his bed. His heart lurched at the scream again, throwing on his breeches he ran barefoot downstairs towards the kitchen where the screams came from.

Stopping at the door the view before him was puzzling.

"Helmsley there it is catch it," she screamed perched on a table with a skillet in her hand. Flour was everywhere. The scene was amusing, but funny.

She screamed with a frantic nervous giggle as she pointed to the far corner while poor old Helmsley tried to get closer.

"What on earth is going on here?" Dominic asked.

Helmelsy turned to look at him and the sight of the poor man looked shameless, he had flour all over him that he looked like a ghost.

"Forgive me m'lord... but we have a visitor, we are trying to get rid of." He shyly explained right before poor Emilia screamed and made him jump.

Rolling his eyes, he walked calmly into the kitchen towards the table, pulled the skillet out of Emilia's hand and quickly pulled her off the table into his arms. She was skittish and frightened. Peeping over the table, he looked to see what had her in such a state. His eyes bulged at the size of the rat that was scurrying to the corner. Bloody hell he was big!

Quickly he put her back on the table and walked over to join Helmsley in the battle.

The show she watched unfold was a fiasco at its best. Helmsley and Dominic turned the kitchen upside down. Now he was miffed that their efforts of catching the hideous rodent turned into a laughing matter for Emilia, who was still perched on the table in a fit of laughter watching them throw pots and pans at it. The final showdown proved victorious when finally the last pot that hit it, killed it.

Heavily breathing, exhausted and bothered he turned to face Emilia sprawled on the table in a fit of giggles laughing at them.

She looked stunning. He breathed and swallowed hard just imagining her just like this in his bed after making love to her. He had to look away. She was a torment to him with each day that passed. Her innocent naivety of her exotic beauty ate little by little of his control and the will power to not ravish her. His cock jumped at the way she sat up before him, pulled him closer and wiped the flour from his hair and cheek. She was clueless to his hungry need of her. This barefooted little pixie was his undoing.

Chapter 8

The day was a good day and went its course until the night and all turned in for bed. The slow sound of bad weather rolled in late in the night. She lay awake listening to the clap of thunder and the rain that pelted on the window. It was the worst she had ever heard. The room was dark with only but a few lightning strikes that lit it up. Hunkering down further into the pillows didn't help the pounding of her heart, she was terribly frightened and she was not going to sleep with this noise. Nervously she sat up, her fear took the best of her. The loud rumble ended with a clap that had her bolting out of the room through the hall to Dominic's room.

She quickly walked through the dark room to his bed. Her heart clamored in her chest so hard she felt faint. Frantically, she shook him.

A low moan came from him.

"Dominic please, wake up, " she begged.

"I am scared." She whispered.

He moaned and opened his eyes.

"Emilia!" he drowsily moaned her name.

Scooting over he pulled aside the covers and she climbed in. Shaking as she curled up next to him. He pulled her closer and buried his face into her hair.

Wanting his warmth, she snuggled closer.

She felt so safe, she let her body drift away to sleep.

She came to him in his dreams. He pulled her into his bed and hugged her close. The feel of her body close to his sent him spiraling into a pleasurable abyss. He nuzzled his head into her neck. Her sweet smell wafted his senses and he kissed her neck, then her cheek...Then her lips. He pulled her closer and she gasped. His lips tasted hers and the kiss deepened. She stiffened as his tongue slipped between her parted lips and she quivered beneath him.

She lay still in shock as he moaned her name and deepened the kiss. The taste and smell of whisky on his lips lingered with each kiss that was so sweet. He pulled her closer to his warm body. His chest was bare, his arms muscular. She kissed him with the same intensity and it shook her to the core. Her hands trailed his muscular arms and broad shoulders. This was something unknown to her and her heart raced with this new feeling growing inside of her. The place between her thighs began to twitch and she gasped. His head dipped low and he kissed down her chest.

He pulled her chemise open and exposed her breasts. He squeezed, kissed and sucked them. His hand squeezed and caressed her thigh. She felt his warm hot hands caress and squeeze her buttocks. His hands warm and determined went between her legs and touched her where no one ever had. She quivered beneath his strokes, squeezing her eyes shut to the intense fire growing in her body. This, she thought, was a dream. A dream cruelly playing with her senses, if it was she did not want to wake up. The warmth of his lips caressed her cheek and slid to her ears. His hot breathe whispered things he wanted to do to her and her insides tightened.

She was wet for him as he stroked and circled the soft bud between her thighs her hips bucked. She whimpered with his fingertips stroking her. She could feel the hardness of his manhood on her thighs. Gently he rolled above her and continued to kiss her. She was lost in the heated passion of it all that the danger flag never raised. In the throes of this sexual exploration, she didn't know of, she instinctively opened her legs. He cradled himself between her legs, the bulk of his cock throbbed as he pressed it to her wetness. The barrier between them was driving her crazy. She writhed beneath him as he undid his breeches and positioned his self to enter her. The frenzied feeling of it all caught her breath when he pressed his warm thick shaft harder.

She pulled away frightened with a gasp his name on her breath.

"Dominic!" she whimpered.

He stopped.

Something in this dream of his was a little more real than anything. The panting and heavy breathing came to his ear. Opening his eyes, he blinked repeatedly trying to clear his dazed mind.

The vision before him made his heart skit to halt. He looked into eyes glazed with passion.

Leaning back on his knees, he looked at Emilia.

Her breasts in full view and chemise hitched up to her waist, exposing her lower body.

Her chest rose and fell quickly his cock jumped at how her breasts quivered with each breath.

"Emilia?" He croaked in disbelief.

Sitting bolt upright, she looked at him still breathless and dazed .

Her hair billowed around her face. She looked every bit of a girl properly kissed and nearly fucked.

With a moan, he neared the edge of the bed and buried his face in his hands.

What the bloody hell did he do?

He was so close. He nearly did the unthinkable and it felt so right.

He sat silent with his back to her; of their own free will, her hands caressed his shoulders. Trembling, she came closer to him. She wanted to feel him close to her again. She caressed him from behind. Her lips gently kissed his shoulder, then his neck. He immediately lost his train of thought. She wanted him so much she could not control her need for him. Soft, delicate fingers caressed his chest while lips trailed the saltiness of his neck.

He reached up to caress her head and turned to meet the sweetness of her lips. The enticing feel of her muddled his mind and good judgment, which at the moment was of no use to either of them. Like liquid warmth to his skin, he pulled her around into his lap. They continued their kisses with wild abandonment; his hand caressed and grazed every inch of her. The warmth of her skin beneath his hands made him crave more of her.

With a fierce possession of her lips, he kissed her hard. Her whimpers only made his cock harder. With a growl in his throat, he swung with her in his arms and laid her back on the bed. He looked at her, her eyes were gorgeous because the passion she felt for him was clear in them. He claimed her lips again crushing her petite lush body with his. Her warmth, smell and softness where driving him mad. He dropped back to reality with a heavy breath, he pulled for self-control. Any other scoundrel would have jumped at this opportunity. But, she was a virgin, a child at best and inexperienced. He could not do this to her.

He stood quickly with his back to her.

She slowly slid from the bed.

Still on shaky legs, breathing heavily, dizzy, and still tingling between her legs she stood silently behind him

She inched closer to touch him, but he pulled away.

Raking his fingers thru his hair, he turned to look at her, she looked tousled as if just recently bedded, her lips dewy and red from their kisses.

"It's best if you go to your room." His voice trembled.

"Dominic." Her voice was barely audible.

Closing his eyes to the sound of her voice just rolled off his skin like decadent silk and he moaned.

Confused, she stood not moving.

"Just go,...... please." His voice harshly rose.

"But, I don't understand" She cried.

"What don't you understand out of all of this Emilia? Other than that I nearly had sex with you." His voice was harsh.

"You're only 16, you're only a child an inexperienced, naive child," his voice harshly rose.

She flinched. Shaking her head not wanting to hear him, she turned and ran out of his room.

His words hurt more than anything did. She lay there in a daze as if she received the hardest slap across her face. He thought she was a child. She hated herself for what she did. She should have never done this, she felt dirty and ashamed. She turned her face into her pillow and just cried until her heart could not take anymore.

He stood there by her door wanting to go to her. Her cries were the worst that tugged at his heart. He didn't mean to hurt her. Before he could stop himself, the words were said. He felt like such an idiot, how could he have said it. Couldn't you have been gentler you fool? He berated himself.

He battled with the decision that they had to return. If he did not she would be in his bed by nightfall. He could not do this to her. Early that morning he sent for the carriage and gave Helmsley strict instructions on what he must do. He gave her the news that they were leaving the next morning and she didn't protest. Her face was void of any expression.

Chapter 9

She descended the stairs in a beautiful dress ready for their return. He watched her give Helmsley a hug. His face as sad as can be with her departure. He entered the carriage and sat before her. He looked at her and he could see she did not sleep at all. She looked miserable and he was kicking himself because he knew he was the cause of it and feeling the same way.

Deep down inside his mind told him it was for the best that she kept him at arm's length, it was better for them both. Soon she will be attending balls and dinners to meet a proper suitor, she would get married and he would go on living his usual bachelor life. She needed to understand this. And reluctantly he had to convince her.

He leaned closer and looked at her lowered gaze. For a moment, he thought of what to say to ease this awkwardness between them.

He gently pulled her hands and held on to them.

"Emilia, look at me." He spoke softly.

She hesitated, then obediently she looked into his eyes.

"I want you to forgive me for what happened." He pleaded.

"I was severely out of line. None of it was your fault. Do you understand?"

Quickly she nodded.

"I want to apologize as well m'lord," she replied.

He looked deep into her eyes and his heart dipped at her words.

"Whatever for, beautiful?" His eyes softened and he rubbed her hands that began to shake.

Licking her lips, she looked down.

"It is known that it is a lady's duty to act properly and to be respectful at all times. My smiles and sweet gestures provoked you, for that I apologize." She whispered.

He saw tears threatening to fall as she practically blamed herself for it all.

Amazed at her response, he edged closer and spoke to her with a serious stare full of meaning.

"You have nothing to be blamed for. I.... Overstepped my boundaries Emilia."

"You trusted me and I abused that trust. It will never happen again." He whispered.

Why make promises you cant keep? Rake!!!

His soul was surely going to hell. He was beyond redemption.

Deep down, he wanted her with a desperation that terrified him.

She tried to tell herself, what she felt last night was a weakness, a simple betrayal of her body responding to something forbidden. The urge that grew in her was overwhelming. It was obvious he was attracted to her, that much was whispered to her between his kisses.

She desired him and she had to simply deal with the truth. It just simply could not be!!!

*****

They entered London and the bustling, busy streets pulled into view. He watched as her eyes looked through the window and her look turned very sad.

Her hands began to twirl a handkerchief handed to her by Helmsley.

The carriage pulled up to a beautiful cobblestone home, fenced with a luscious lawn and landscape.

Nervously she sat still, not moving. He leaned forward and placed his hand above her's. Her eyes met his and she fell apart before him. Nervously she shook her head, looked through the window, and looked at him.

"I cannot go in there." She panicked with tears falling.

He held her gaze with so much concern.

He gently tilted her chin up and smiled.

"You are not alone, I will go in with you." His voice was reassuring

The door to the carriage opened and he stepped out first. Her trembling hands took his and she stepped down. Head down, she led the way up the stairs to the front door. She paused for a while and turned to face him. Sad eyes looked up at him that spoke of what she felt.

He caressed her cheek and gave a smile.

"You can do this."

Looking up into his eyes she searched his. Her eyes began to tear.

"I want to go back to Grisham." Her lips quivered.

His heart ached with her plea.

"In a heart beat beautiful I would take you to the end of the universe if I could." He wanted so much to tell her.

Resignation was his only option. She wasn't for him.

Slowly he pulled her hands to his and squeezed them.

"You have nothing to fear beautiful," he assured her.

With that said, she slowly turned, took a deep shaky breath and raised her hand to the large round brass ring on the door and gave three knocks.

They stood and waited until the latch of the door clicked and it opened.

The straight face of a butler appeared at the door.

His eyes softened with a fatherly concerned glare when he glanced at her.

"Hello Jeoffry," her voice was soft and quietly spoken.

"Emilia dear child, you have returned," His astonished look turned happy with joy to see her.

She walked into his open arms and received a tight warm hug.

Dominic smiled. He felt the care the butler had for her and that eased his worries.

He bid them to enter.

A maid came into view, her eyes widened.

"Emilia!" Tears welled up in her eyes.

She was a very pretty blonde with blue eyes. Knowing who he was immediately, she curtsied.

"M'lord"

The commotion at the front entrance began with all the servants piled up at the door welcoming her home. The prattle and worry of her disappearance was repeated more than once.

The deep voice of a man was heard from the far end of the house that made them scurry off to where they came.

She stepped back into Dominic when the man with the loud voice came into view. He was stocky, short and had a stern look on his face. Dominic placed strong hands on Emilia's shoulders as she backed up crushing his toes.

He walked into their view.

He never looked at Dominic. The loving, caring image of a worried guardian was not in his eyes, the welcoming hug never came. In shock, Dominic watched as his lips curled into a snarl and he backhanded Emilia so hard she fell to the floor. He yanked her up by the arm she had injured and she let out such a scream. He quickly let go only to see that Dominic flew into a rage and stood before Emilia. He grabbed the man by the shirt and drew him close to meet the deadly glare of blue steel before slamming his fist into the man's face.

"Don't you ever put your hands on her again," Dominic roared.

He let the man go, sending him flying back, he toppled into a nearby flower vase in a crash to the floor.

Kneeling beside her, he held her close checking her shoulder, he lifted her face to see the trail of blood coming from her mouth. Quickly he pulled out his handkerchief and wiped at it. Helping her up, he held her trembling body close to him.

"Now I understand her fear of returning here," he breathed.

Watching her uncle stand and wipe the blood from his mouth and nose.

"You are going to pay for this," her uncle warned.

"That will have to wait old man; what's more important is the well being of your niece, Don't you think?" Dominic's eyes were daggers at this moment.

His anger seemed to make the Duke recollect his rage a bit and calm down.

"Speak your piece, then get the hell out of my house, McAllister. "

An eyebrow shot up in Dominic's eye.

"Yes, I know who you are, you bloody bastard. A scoundrel in sheep's clothing," The duke squeezed his fists until they were white.

"Can we speak in private?" Dominic asked, expecting no other answer but a yes.

Fuming the duke bellowed for Gertrude and Sarah to attend to Emilia and urged Dominic to follow him to his study.

He watched Emilia's uncle take a seat But, refused to sit down himself. He stood looking at the burly old man.

"Do you care to tell me how my niece ended up in your company, McAllister" he folded his hands sitting back waiting for an explanation.

Breathing slowly he tried to control his anger. Dominic flexed his hands on the top of a chair separating him from the Duke, not much of a barrier but it would give the fool some time to run if need be.

Bowing his head, he continued.

"I was on my way to Grisham, my estate and I found her injured on my boat"

Her uncle sat up straight with a frown.

"She was naked, with a dislocated shoulder and two broken ankles."

"What? How could that be?" The duke questioned perplexed by such news.

"I don't know, but, however this happened it was meant for her to be left for dead or never found again."

Silently the Duke sat and took all what Dominic had said.

Then immediately he shot Dominic an angry glare.

"So this whole time she was with you, alone and unchaperoned." He watched the old man's anger rise.

"Yes, forgive me if I did not send for someone sooner, for the naked girl child with no identity found injured in my boat." He sarcastically hissed.

"If you layed one hand on her, McAllister, so help me..." The duke fumed.

"I can assure you she is untouched." He quickly hissed.

Bloody liar, every inch of your lips and hands were on her!!!

The skeptical look turned into semi-relief on the Duke's stare as he sat back and looked away from Dominics scrutinizing eyes.

"Please, save the theatrics old man, you know good and well her virtue is only an important chess piece in your game to throw her to some lout or lovesick schoolboy that can take her off your hands," Dominic yelled.

"How dare you speak to me that way." In an offensive glare he stood abruptly from his seat.

"Yes, I dare. You don't have to worry and play the doting uncle worried for the well being of his niece." Dominic began to pace furiously.

"Get out! I don't need to hear anymore of your preposterous accusations."

"That is fine with me old man, but know this. If anything happens to Emilia, even so much if a scratch falls upon her. You better believe you will have me to answer to." Dominic warned.

"Are you threatening me?" he growled.

The duke's face turned red as an apple.

"M'lord duke, consider it a warning with considerable consequence if not heeded." With that last note, Dominic turned and stormed off to leave.

Walking towards the front door, he heard Emilia call his name.

"Dominic!" Her voice meek and soft.

He turned and quickly blinked, looking up at her, his eyes softened and the anger he felt quickly went away. It was a total transformation of her, she looked stunning.

She slowly stepped down the stairs and walked over to him.

Their eyes connected for a while. He held her hands and kissed them both.

"Will I ever see you again?" She asked, worried.

He smiled and tapped her nose.

"I am not going too far. If you need me for anything I will be here."

Her eyes sparkled and her smile was wide that her pearly teeth just lit up her face.

He caressed her cheek, his heart just melted when she closed her eyes, raised her hand to squeeze his hand to her cheek. He gently bent his head and kissed her forehead.

"Stay out of trouble." He tapped her nose.

She nodded with a coy smile. Misty green eyes watched him turn to walk out the front door with one last glance her way he winked at her and it brought a smile that made her blush.

The door clicked shut and her tears fell. She turned and met the stern gaze of her uncle. With head bent, she turned to walk back upstairs to her room.

The short carriage ride home was rewarding because he hungered for his bed, he was exhausted and bothered. He met Bufford's warm, welcoming smile at the entrance way.

"M'lord it is good to see you again."

Dominic nodded.

"Good to see you too, Bufford" he smiled.

He entered into the foyer handed his coat and cravat to Bufford.

"M'lord, would you like me to fetch you a drink?"

"I'll have some whiskey in the study," He replied.

With a quick nod, Bufford walked off.

He entered the study and threw his self in a large chair by the window. His body weary and exhausted thought back to the day he had.

Bufford entered a while later with a glass of whiskey. Before he turned away, Dominic asked.

"Bufford, did I get any messages while I was gone?"

Clearing his throat, he came closer and stood near him.

"Indeed you did m'lord, would you like me to relay them?"

Dominic nodded his head, sat quietly, and listened to the messages of who came to visit. He took a sip while hearing Bufford rambled on and concentrated on the last interesting message from his latest companion in the boudoir.

"Lady Hannah went on to say, m'lord, that she could not wait for your return so you can plunge your manhood into her nether regions..." Dominic choked sputtering and coughing on his whiskey while Bufford non ceremoniously thwacked him repeatedly on his back. Bufford cleared his throat "Shall I continue m'lord?"

Still breathing heavily and trying to clear his airway, Dominic shook his head.

Slouching back, he breathed in deeply wiping the stinging tears from his eyes..

Oh! Hannah never seemed to amaze him. She was a lioness in bed and he couldn't wait to get to her either, he chuckled. But, then he grew silent. Emilia came to his thoughts. With a large sigh, he leaned forward and closed his eyes, then buried his hands in his face. With a deep moan and curse, he stood and walked to lean against the window.

Concerned Bufford stood behind him.

"M'lord is something wrong? Are you well?"

He stood silent for a while.

"Bufford, the night I left to Grisham Estate on my way there I found an injured young girl on my boat."

"Injured, m'lord?" Bufford surprised by the news came closer.

"She was badly injured and naked, crying for help. She had a dislocated shoulder and two broken ankles." His voice low.

"My Heavens!" Bufford gasped.

"The whole time I've been gone, I cared for her until she got better." Dominic turned to sit on the windowsill and face Bufford.

"Bufford, the weeks we spent in each other's company, something grew between us, you have no idea of how free I felt." He smiled at the memories.

"Is it possible M'lord, you are smitten with her." Bufford asked, looking at Dominic in a different light.

"No...Bufford, there is more to it. Underneath her demure and shy nature, there is this beautiful free willed girl that evokes a feeling in me I cannot name. I dream about her. When I look into her eyes, I completely melt."

Bufford stood silently waiting for Dominic to continue.

"The hardest thing for me was to return her to her family."

"So she is with her family, M'lord?" Bufford questioned wanting to know more about the young girl that has completely besotted his employer.

"She is Worthington's niece, The Duke of Margave." Dominic's lips curled in anger.

"Oh my, I see!" Bufford whispered, knowing too well of the Dukes ways.

"The bastard never even tended a caring look of concern towards her, he right away slapped her before me." Dominic's anger rose.

Knowing Dominic detests mistreatment of a woman, he swallowed nervously. After hearing that the girl was unchaperoned and alone with him and nearly beating the duke to a bloody pulp, he feared the worst.

"He did not call you out, did he Milord?" Holding on to fear itself, he clenched the silver platter in his hand.

Shaking his head Dominic looked away.

"No, but, I wish he did."

"I promised her I would be there for her if she needed anything. And I tend to keep that promise, Bufford"

The silence that followed was indication for him to retreat.

"Bufford?"

He stopped to look at Dominic.

"Yes, M'lord."

The look in Dominic's eyes was one he had never seen before.

"If a beautiful young lass comes looking for me by the name of Emilia, don't turn her away. She is welcome here any time." The boyish smile that rose to his face was astounding.

Bufford gave a humble smile and nodded.

"Most definitely, as you wish M'lord."

Turning Bufford walked out of the study and closed the door behind him. With a smile, the mysterious beauty, intrigued him. There was still hope for his lord yet. He had to get this man married quickly because his life was spiraling out of control with these so-called ladies or much better, harlots in fine clothing. They had no shame; he shook his head and rolled his eyes upward. He sighed, closing his eyes, giving himself the sign of the cross, he gestured a prayer upwards for enlightenment on his efforts.

Dominic finally retired to his room. A little after a few seconds of placing his head on his pillow, he fell fast asleep with her on his mind.

******

Dominic woke up with her on his mind and he gasped. His shaft was thick with need for her. His dreams of her felt so vivid, that raw lust took over his imaginations and in his dreams, her lush body lay beneath him soft, sweet and responsive. He groaned in agony, wrapping his hands around his throbbing cock. Her scent a stamp on his memory, played erotically with his senses. How he wished her to be in this bed with him. Pumping his fists up and down on his shaft he needed to release some sexual tension. She tantalized and aroused him in his dreams and the wave of pleasure showered over him with each stroke. He shuddered from the force of his release, laying weak and still unsatisfied against his pillows. He wanted her.

Chapter 10

The expanse of a week had gone, and everything returned to normal. Dominic sat and listened to Bufford's morning gossip candidly while pouring his tea. On strict orders, he was to check on the well-being of Emilia. All of his attention was on him when he relayed his messages about how she was doing.

"She is doing well, M'lord" Bufford nodded.

Dominic smiled to himself. He missed the little imp and her sweet ways. Thank goodness her return did not warrant suspicion or gossip, for that he was relieved.

"Are you going to visit her today M'lord?" Bufford asked.

Dominic sat back and smiled.

"Yes, Bufford I am."

With that said, Dominic ordered that the carriage pick him up.

His visits made her days much better. She had a radiant smile that just lit up her eyes when he visited. They went for a stroll throughout the garden with Sarah and Gertrude trailing not too far behind.

They giggled and whispered in awe of the sight of Emilia and Dominic together. There was no mistaking an attraction was evident between the two of them.

They walked over to a large oak tree and talked. He leaned against it and listened while she talked about her day. He looked down at the top of her head shiny dark brown tresses curled to her shoulder. He loved the way she wore it loose with bouncy curls. She looked up at him, smiled, and covered her face as she continued explaining her mischievous makings for the day.

During her piano lesson the piano somehow, inexplicably was missing a cord. Therefore, a tune was out of place and sadly, her lessons were canceled.

He chuckled and tapped her nose.

"You were gloating were you not?"

Coyly she looked away pointing up her nose.

"Au contraire M'lord, I gave my most saddened pitiful stare, and I cried." Her green eyes met his astonished gaze.

He shook his head laughing, he stared into green eyes that glistened with mirth.

"You are a little hellion!" he turned and leaned his back against the tree and folded his arms. He continued looking at her.

She impishly smiled and gave him a mock curtsey admitting that she was.

Such action had Dominic in a state of laughter that he pulled her close into a deep hug.

"Goodness, you light up anyone's day."

He pulled her hand into his arm, and they turned to walk back to the garden.

"M'lord?" Emilia looked up at him.

He looked down into her eyes.

"Are you going to the Wakefield ball?" She asked.

He scrunched his nose and looked into her beseeching stare. Her eyes went soft with wanting him to go.

He sighed.

He knew she did not like going to those affairs, but deep down, if he attended she will most likely go as well.

"I suppose I can go for a scant moment. Besides, I want to dance with the belle of the ball." He silently watched her eyes lower at his words, a sign of sadness in her eyes at the thought of him dancing with the belle of the ball and not her saddened her.

Such a look warmed his heart.

"Oh!" she whispered, looking away.

A teasing grin tugged at his lips.

"Emilia?"

She looked up at him with sad eyes.

"The belle of the ball is you."

He leaned down, kissed her forehead, and was rewarded with a smile and two pink cheeks.

*****

The Wakefield Ball

It was the event decked in all of its opulence and grandeur not a soul could miss it. The ballroom flaunted its occupants in their most elegant attire.

Nervously, Emilia flanked on the right side of her uncle's arm, and her aunt on his left followed the crowd entering the doorway. The crowd looked at the beautiful girl entering that caught the attention of many young men.

Her eyes lowered,after she smiled and curtsied her way in.

Her uncle passed her into her aunt's arm to walk in order to greet the rest of the guests while he stood talking to other gentlemen.

Her eyes looked around and spotted the eyes of onlookers looking at her, a few tipped their glasses of wine to her, and she returned a smile.

Her eyes continued to watch the few dancers and inconspicuously search the crowd for Dominic until she found him. Her heart slipped its normal rhythm. He was as gorgeous as they come. He was dressed all in black; none could compare to his masculine beauty. She watched as another man equal in stature and very handsome as well pointed him in her direction. He turned, and their eyes finally met. Nervously she licked her lips and smiled.

He gave her the most gorgeous smile that made her legs weak.
*****

He stood talking with his good friend Dimitri in the middle of the conversation he faltered.

"Oh! My who is that tender morsel?" Dimitri turned Dominic to look at the one in question.

His eyes saw the elegant, gorgeous sequined lavender dress. He looked into the most mesmerizing eyes. Emilia was breathtaking, a budding beauty that he wanted to pluck for himself.

With a smile, he looked at Dimitri and gave a wide smile.

"That my brother is Emilia Westham." With interest, Dimitri held her gaze and Dominic followed it. Clearing his throat, he put a wide grin on his face and pat Dimitri on the back.

"Unfortunately for you, she is unavailable because you are getting married," He smirked.

And I would break your jaw if you went anywhere near her!

With a grin and a sigh, Dimitri shook his head.

"One can only dream my friend. One can only dream."

Turning, he agreed silently and watched as young girls circled around her and began to giggle and look their way. It was obvious they were talking about him and Dimitri. Nevertheless, his eyes never left hers. He gave a seductive wink and raised his glass to them as they began to squeal with delight and hide their smiles behind their gloved hands. She knew it was meant only for her, and she sweetly smiled at him and gave the most endearing blush.

The night went by in a flash before her as she was twirled and spun around the room. Flattering words were spoken to her, and the most coquettish smiles were given to her as well. However, none mattered to her, but his. When he finally took her into his arms, no one else in the room existed. His touch and stronghold had her floating. They danced and smiled at each other. Ever so often, he would say something that would brighten her eyes, and she in change would give a reply that would pull a chuckle or two and a breathtaking grin.

"I do say beautiful one, you have every young buck in here vying for your attention." He smiled down at her.

She looked up at him and returned a sweet beautiful grin.

"Is that a bad thing m'lord?" She asked with an innocent stare.

His noes wrinkled mockingly.

" I do say some of them look awful, others look questionable, and a good few have a tarnished reputation." He pulled a soft laugh from her that made her eyes sparkle.

"M'lord, you are wicked," she whispered hiding her smile.

He cocked his head to the side and looked down into her eyes curiously.

"So, has anyone of them caught your eyes yet, little one?"

With a meek smile, she caught his eyes in a stare that quickened his heart.

"Yes, M'lord" She whispered dreamily.

"Really, that was fast" He cocked an eyebrow

" For curiosity's sake, may I have his name?" he gave a wry smile.

Yes, the scoundrel that caught your attention so I can choke him.

With a grin that lit up her eyes, she held his gaze for a while and shook her head with a mischievous grin.

"No, but I can tell you m'lord, he is the most gorgeous man I have ever seen."

A sudden dip in his heart caught him by surprise to hear her describe any man in that fashion.

She continued to look into his eyes and watched his eyes deepen in color to her words. A sign that he was displeased with her response, but he hid it very well.

"M'lord?" she looked deep into his eyes.

As the dance was slowly coming to an end she quickly whispered to him squeezing his palm gently.

"That man is you." Her eyes immediately hid the desire she felt for him for their sake of anyone watching them.

Caught off guard by her response, he quickly recollected his self and chuckled. Holding her hands together, he kissed them with a wink and seductive smile.

" I am off limits, little one." He shook his head with a seductive grin.

She looked up at him with a smile, the light in her eyes held his gaze that made him grin from ear to ear.

"True, but in my dreams, you are not." She wrinkled her nose in a teasing manner.

She was every bit the saucy one, he mused with a chuckle.

"You naughty Minx," he grinned with desire twinkling in his gaze. He leaned forward and whispered. "Neither in mine."

The dreamlike stare she gave him was beautiful. The color of her eyes immediately went a couple of shades darker with his response. Satisfied with her reaction, he watched her cheeks turn a vibrant pink before watching her being pulled into a circle of her friends.

*****

To the ordinary eyes that watched them gracefully dance together; it was a modest courteous dance, she gifted him. However, to the jealous eye that watched them, there was much more seen between the two of them... A budding a romance? Maybe...But not for long.

Lady Hannah stood and watched her lover dance with the young girl. With jealously she observed her and could tell she was beautiful. She had every man watching her some as jealous as she because she was dancing with Dominic. She impatiently watched the two smile and laugh as he gracefully twirled her around. The sickening coos and awes were bothering her greatly, only the fake plastered smile on her face never gave away her disdain she felt for the girl.

The dance continued and all enjoyed the merriment. Sometime in between dances, she managed to turn away one or two young men to rest her feet. Curious as to where Dominic had run off to, she went in search of some refreshment and then search for him.

In a secluded alcove, Dominic and Lady Hannah hid and began their efforts to appease each other's growing need in their loins he for Emilia and she for him. Their hushed moans were drowned out by the loud music. He avoided her lips not wanting to kiss her, he began to dutifully roam her body with his hands. He took her ample breasts and squeezed each one with no satisfaction.

He pressed her up against the wall, raised her thighs around his waist, and pumped his cock into her with so much force she gasped. His mind wandered to the night Emilia came to his bed. His groin pulsed with the vision of her in his head. A part of him regretted letting her go. How he would have loved to be with her and caress her lush body.

His mind was brought back from his lusty daydreaming to the present the moment his release came. Spent and panting, he put Hannah down and began to fix himself. He didn't look at her as she fixed her breasts back into her bodice and arranged herself.

As they began to leave, Emilia caught sight of them. She watched as the woman turned and leaned in close and gave him a kiss on the cheek. Her heart sank at the sight of them. With that, she turned away and returned to the ballroom.

She put on the perfect smile until they all left.

Exhausted she walked up the stairs. She changed into her chemise and sat at the edge of her bed. All thoughts went to her dance with Dominic.

Her thoughts were filled with erotic images of them. The night she slipped into his bed, she would never forget it. Heat crept up her cheeks at the memory of how he caressed her and whispered his desire for in her ears. Then tonight when she mentioned, it was he who had her attentions, her knees went weak with his twinkling eyes.

He was off limits, he winked.

Drowsily she yawned, content with the night.

She lay back on the soft bed and closed her eyes immediately with his image on her mind. It was his embrace that pulled her close, and his seductive voice that lulled her to sleep.

Chapter 11

T he days were torturous for her because she had to endure so much. She had no sense of peace and she was weary of so much attention from different suitors. She was bothered more because as of late, she saw very little of Dominic and she wanted to see him.

She impatiently waited for everyone to fall asleep. Her best chance to sneak out was now; she nervously sat up and looked around. Her heart slammed in her chest, trying to sneak out was no easy feit.

Breathing the brisk cool air into her shaking lungs calmed her very little.

The brief walk through the park, taking the short cut was fastest. Very few people still roamed the streets at that hour. Standing off to the side near a tree, his home came into view. She was not sure if he was home, or if he would be happy to see her. All she knew was that she had to see him. Tonight.

Shakily legs carried her across the stone walkway to his entrance door.

She stood on the steps to his front door, nervous and queasy, she wanted to turn around but she couldn't. All you have to do is knock. She told herself.

She walked up the stairs and stood before the large cherry oak door and knocked.

After a few seconds the door creaked open and a man in a black suit stepped out to see her.

"Good evening, sir, my name is..." Her soft voice could not finish.

"Lady Emilia how are you?" His face smiled.

Her brows furrowed.

"How do you know my name?"

He smiled and gave her a nod.

"M'lord spoke much about you."

She smiled and looked away immediately turning a slight shade of pink.

Standing aside, he let her pass.

"Please do enter."

She entered into the foyer and looked at the numerous pictures of the McAllister men from the past in elegant portraits lined on the walls.

"M'lady, lord Dominic is in his study if you would like to go up. I must attend to a quick task or I would show you up"

Smiling with her most beautiful smile.

"Thank you, sir, most kind of you. "

He nodded and gave a bow.

"Bufford, milady at your service."

She giggled prettily.

He walked off in a hurry and left her in the large foyer. Slowly she took one step at a time, holding on to the banister that spiraled up the staircase.

Finally getting to the clearing, she came before another picture frame, then a beautiful bust of a female statue holding a harp. The low moan of a male voice startled her. Curious to the noise she followed where it was coming from. The door down the hall to the right was slightly opened and the moan and whispers became more audible.

Coming closer she stood by shocked at what she saw. A naked woman on her knees in the big poster bed facing her, bouncing up and down moaning. Shyly Emilia looked down at herself aware that she had smaller breasts than the ample ones the woman had. She was voluptuous.

They jiggled and bounced with her movement. Her heart skidded to halt when manly hands reached for them and squeezed them. Quickly he sat up and caressed her. Immobile she stood there and her eyes met the lustful gaze of Lady Hannah, the Duke of Cramwell's wife. Her heart dropped to her stomach when she watched the duchess smile wickedly back at her. In the throes of passion, she continued to bounce and moan his name.

"Oh! Dominic!" She whimpered in a squeal.

Not wanting to see anymore her tears fell free she stopped at the stair case hands on her stomach as if she were kicked in it. Holding on to the banister tightly she continued down the stairs in a run.

Weeping and crying, she passed a puzzled Bufford and walked right out the door without looking back.

Blinded by the tears she made it home. Slowly she trudged up the stairs weak, heartbroken and in tears. She slipped into her room where she threw herself on her bed and cried into her pillow. Wracked with tears she wept until she had no more strength to stay awake.

The next morning he awoke refreshed and renewed. Dominic carried out his day busily as he handled daily work. He sat back in his chair. It's been a while since he saw Emilia, with him being busy and her daily lessons it was hard to get some time alone with her. Pretty soon he would not get any time with her because suitors are being sought after for marriage. The idea did not sit well with him; he wanted to be the only one in her life. He smiled to himself remembering their first dance at the ball. She was graceful, every bit the beauty of the ball and no doubt every man's desire. A slight tinge of jealousy settled with him as he watched her swirl, sway and smile with some of the beau's.

He decided to go visit her.

****

"Again, Emilia!" The stern voice of Madam Georgette ordered.

The morning piano lessons were grating on her nerves. No sleep made her edgy, agitated ,weary and her heart if she still had some remnants of it left barely beat because it ached so much. Her eyes blurred with tears that could barely see the black and white keys before her. She barely paid attention to her surroundings, with her mind wandering off to what she saw. Over and over her mind played the images of them making love. She stopped playing mid note the overwhelming feeling in her heart was too great and she couldn't contain it any longer. Her tears fell free and she cried. Her tears splashed on the piano keys like rain drops from the sky.

He watched from the entrance of the solar her back to him as she strummed the keys off tune. Her shoulders slumped and she paused. He watched as the heavyset woman beside her impatiently tapped the piano and ridiculed her for slouching. Something wasn't right, he noticed. She began to weep. Holding back, he watched the woman tap hard on Emilia's hand and tap her back again to sit up straight.

His anger rose at her harsh treatment.

With a loud thwack of the stick on the Piano, it made her jump as well as he.

"Sit up Emilia" She scowled.

It was her breaking point. Immediately all of her just unable to take any more just cracked under the pressure.

They all jumped at her blood-curdling scream.

"Enough" She stood abruptly facing her.

"Hit me one more time with that bloody stick you cow, I swear I will choke the life out of you," she screamed in a cry.

He watched in awe as Emilia pounced on the woman yanking the stick from her and cracking it in half slamming it to the floor.

With a frightened gasp, the woman stepped back terrified.

Seething with rage, she never felt the harsh arms around her waist, keeping her from actually pummeling the woman.

Feral eyes never left the old women forcing her to retreat running scared.

She pulled away from him. Red eyes filled with tears looked up at him. Ashamed that he witness such a display, she turned away from him and she walked off.

"Emilia?" He called her.

She ran up the stairs. He took two at a time behind her and managed to get through the door, she was trying to close in his face.

He walked in more bothered than anything at her behavior. She turned her back to him.

"Do you mind telling me what happened downstairs?" He breathed.

She stayed silent for a while her body still trembling with anger.

"Go away, " she cried softly.

"Not until you answer me, What is wrong?" He asked.

He gently spoke to her not able to understand her sudden outburst of anger.

"What is wrong is that I am tired. I am tired of all of this. The lessons, the balls, the soirees, I want to be far away from here..." She cried.

Far away from you !!!

He pulled her into his arms.

"Look at me, Emilia" He whispered.

Her demeanor changed.

Her eyes held a sadness he could not explain.

Not realizing it until it was done, she quickly wrapped her fingers around his neck, pulled him close and kissed him. What drove her to this bold move? She did not know, but it was too late. He stiffened, broke the kiss and held her at arm's length. There was something in her eyes. Desperation? Wanting? Lust? Her boldness was rewarded, because he pulled her close and kissed her back. Innocence and sweetness branded his lips with so much need.

She completely took him by surprise. He gently ran his fingers up her back and caressed her.

The sweet feeling of passion was building up between them. His kisses deepened.

With a groan, he had her up against a nearby wall. He quickly lifted her up and wrapped her legs around his waist. Like pieces of a puzzle that fit their perfect match is how she felt cradled on his waist.

Warm, strong hands caressed soft silky thighs as he ground his hard cock against her. Her gasps and sweet moan set him on fire. This sensual act of abandon was part of the tales she would hear the woman whisper about. It was forbidden and wrong, but yet so good and right.

A need for him grew between her legs. His head dipped low, kissed her neck and sucked her ear, smiling when she moaned softly and sweetly his name. He wove his fingers through her hair.

She broke away from his kiss.

He saw the look in her eyes.

"Make love to me, Dominic," she whispered close to his lips.

He stiffened at her request. Still in the throes of passion he kissed her again. Ready for this moment more than ever he moaned and placed his forehead to hers. Closing his eyes, he hissed a curse.

Gently he let her loose to stand.

He met her glazed over eyes filled with so much want he had to look away.

"What is wrong?" her eyes confused, looked up at him.

"I can't." He rasped.

"Why?" Tears began to fill her eyes.

"It would ruin you and any chances of you getting married," he whispered.

He turned away.

"I don't care about that," she cried.

"But I do." He hissed.

Silently, he watched the passion slip from her gaze and turn to anger. Her green eyes turned a few shades light and feral. For a moment time stood still as she looked at him.

"You can bed that whore of the Duchess, that is married, But I'm only good for stolen kisses is that right!" She cried.

Before she could take those words back, something in Dominic's stare made her nervously step back. His jaw clenched. He pulled her close until they were nose to nose.

"That whore as you so call her is experienced in things you know little about. I don't bed inexperienced little girls," He hissed.

Her soft palm met the roughness of his jaw with a hard slap.

"Get out!" She cried.

Just a sting to him, but it was more of a blow to the stomach to her. His nose flared and his gaze turned to ice. A tremor betrayed her defiant stand when he pulled her close and slammed her body to his.

His lips came down on hers hard, his arm tight around her waist. He pulled her against the wall, his kisses deepened. Merciless, rough strong hands squeezed her thigh all the way up to her rump. Immediately they found their way in between the very fabric that was a barrier. His warm, strong hand found what they were looking for and her heart roared. Briefly, he pulled away, then trailed kisses over her neck, smiling that his lips could feel her racing pulse. His fingers rubbed her until she was wet and ready. Her whimpers were shaky. His fingers worked their magic and her heart skid to halt as he tried to slip a finger inside her. She stiffened and pulled back from his touch. He stopped.

Looking into her eyes, his gaze held a triumphant glare. The very reason for what he said before. She wasn't ready.

It bothered him that it had to come to this.

He pushed away from her.

"Come find me when you are no longer acting like a child," He looked at her.

Her gaze lowered and she began to cry.

With a curse, he walked off. He took two stairs at a time and left.

She threw herself on her bed and wept.

*****

The oncoming days were torture for them both and the ones around them that knew of the silent desire they had for one another, saw their suffering. While she lay awake countless nights crying, he went on endless drunken nights of debauchery. He tried hard to forget her, but he couldn't. She tried hard to forget him as well, But it was the most difficult thing she could do.

Chapter 12

S he sat before her mirror and breathed. She was going to make the most of this night just to get him out of her mind. Her calling card was full and she mustered up the will she lacked and accepted to go to The Cavanaugh's seasonal ball with Lord Evers best known as Adam VanCamp. She eyed the invitation her aunt gave her to read. She would enjoy herself regardless of what she felt at the moment. Sarah dutifully helped her dress with the same sulking look Emilia had. Knowing very well she had no desire to leave or go anywhere.

*****

Dominic sat before the fire throwing back and swallowing down the amber liquid in his glass waiting for it to dull his senses. He scoffed at the invitation Bufford handed him earlier and tossed it on the table before grabbing his glass of whisky. Bufford watched impatiently as Dominic plummeted into an abyss of destruction. He shrugged off the invitation with no interest until he heard that Emilia would be attending and will be escorted by none other but Lord Evers. The ton's most notorious, rake and rich bachelor at that. He

could not think straight with that idea of her being in the company
of that snake. He shot to his feet with a vicious curse and murderous
glare at Bufford. Immediately he dressed in his evening attire and
made his way to The Cavanaugh's.

*****

Entering the main hall, she walked up the stairs to the ballroom.
She smiled prettily at Evers, as he spoke to her. She made little effort
at understanding what he was saying, but pretended to be very interested in his conversations. Not once looked away from him. He
was very handsome and flirtatious. He reveled in the attentions of the
prying eyes of those before them as he entered with her on his arm.
She caught the upturned noses of one or two pretty girls that shot
daggers as she entered. With a nonchalant gaze, she did the same.

*****

He entered with his heart roaring in his ears. Playing off his anger
with a cool smile and nod at those who passed. He had no interest
in small talk, but for courtesy's sake he stood and spoke with one or
two of them.

"McAllister! You rogue where have you been?" The burly voice of
Lord Lockley came into view. Playing off the good humor, he saluted
the old crow that rubbed him the wrong way at times. The cheating
scoundrel could not be trusted not even with a dagger near the back..
The fake grin that plied on Dominic's face with an irritation for the
man. He came closer.

"I do say my man you are in for the latest attraction," He whispered
in a low voice.

He gave a cheerful glance towards the side wall of the ballroom and Dominic followed.

"Isn't she a sight?" he peered at the beautiful young girl in the company of Lord Evers.

Dominic looked at her and she was the loveliest creature he had ever seen. She wore a beautiful peach colored satin gown. His eyes were fixed on the low neckline that hung low and snuggled her breasts. The bodice emphasized her slender waist to perfection. Her hair as always a mass of beautiful dark auburn curls that fell just shy above her waist. She stood out more for that reason she shied away from the norms and styles of the rest.

She exchanged smiles with Evers; often she would give him a beautiful smile. She laughed at something he said, and he gently raised his hands to caress her cheek. She outrageously flirted with him and had no idea what this daring act would eventually lead to. Dominic felt the sudden urge to walk straight to her and drag her away from that bastard. But, the scandal would be too great so he stood leaning against a nearby wall away from the prying eyes and watched her.

Emilia underneath it all played her cards right and she marveled in the grandness of what it was to be the center of attention as many gentlemen flocked to her side. She was swirled around on the dance floor more than once. For a while she was unaware to his presence, until her eyes caught the familiar figure in the corner, as he stood with arms crossed over his chest watching her. Her heart raced when their eyes met and she caught the glimpse of icy blue eyes that looked dangerous .She made it her best effort to ignore him and continued her dance.

He watched as she said something to her last dance partner that she was finally alone. With a quickness, he walked towards her. Her eyes caught his and something in them read danger, but immediately she stood a defiant ground. Slowly he walked towards her.

He silently held out his hand, the glare in his eyes warned her, refusal would not be wise. She lowered her gaze and placed her hands softly in his. He guided her to the floor and held her in his arms.

With a false beam and smile he took her in his arms and whisked her of to the middle of the dance floor.

"I see we wasted no time in finding affections elsewhere," He spoke with an edge of sarcasm to his tone.

She looked up at him and smiled prettily.

"Did you think I would be at home crying for you, M'lord?" she asked with an icy smile that hit its spot.

With a wry smile, he looked down at her. She met his stare with the most taunting smile.

"What? Did you tire of Lady Hannah, or will she be waiting for you elsewhere," Her gaze did not falter. With a smile that shook her to her core, he squeezed her closer.

"Be careful beautiful, you will not like my response," He warned then continued.

"Besides, it is you who should be explaining yourself," He clenched his jaw quickly.

Her eyes held his with a serious glare, and he smirked.

"Why on earth would you let Lord Evers accompany you, don't you realize he is not one to mess with," He looked into her eyes.

"So I have heard, and it is no different from what I have heard about you. Yet I have been alone with you," She shrugged.

"You know very well that is not what I mean Emilia," His voice was dangerously low and she felt his grip tightening.

Emilia smiled mockingly "Are we jealous or worried that he will beat you at compromising my virtue, M'lord?"

She brushed off his dangerous stare and shrugged.

"What I do with it is my concern, m'lord, not yours," she looked away nervously averting his gaze.

With a chuckle, he stared down at her. He stopped in tune at the end of the dance. Quickly, he grasped her hands on his arm and squeezed it. The icy glare followed by a wide grin made her wince. He walked if not pulling her towards the French doors that lead out to the balcony. She nervously stood watching him shut the doors. Licking her lips, she braced herself for what was to come.

Still with his back turned to her and holding on to the door handles he squeezed his eyes shut willing the anger in him to lower. His head swam with choice words to say to her, nothing too brash to hurt her. He let out a breath.

"Why are you doing this, Emilia?" he asked silently.

She lowered her head and gave no answer.

Quickly, he looked at her.

"Is it to provoke me?" He hissed.

"Is it working?" she snapped defiantly with a shaky voice.

She backed away with each of his steps. His nostrils flared and terror crept up her spine. With a harsh squeeze of her arm, she gasped as she slammed into his chest and his arms encircled her waist very tight. He caught her chin in a harsh grip and held her gaze with a warning glare of stormy blue eyes.

"You have much to lose if you get that far," he warned.

"Well, I guess I will just have to try harder then won't I?" She whispered heatedly.

He heard the tremor in her voice. Her eyes looked away from his heated glare.

Her tears fell freely and she began to tremble, shoving against his chest. He squeezed her harder to stop her squirming.

"Let me go. You're hurting me" She cried out.

"No, Emilia you're hurting me, do you have any idea what you are doing to me?" His voice was harsh.

She looked deep into his eyes and returned the same glare. Her breath shook as she spoke.

"I am a child remember? Therefore, no I don't," she retorted.

Fury emanated from his glare and heat from his body. Suddenly, his lips closed over hers with a harsh possession. Demanding entry, her lips parted with his tongue, and the kiss deepened. He caught the taste of her tears on his lips and immediately he stopped. His warm breath touched her lips. "Tread with care in this game you play, Emilia," she looked up into his eyes and caught the glimpse of something new and dangerous.

"Because I don't play fair, nor do I share my winnings."

With those last words, he claimed her lips in a heated kiss once more. He walked off through the ballroom collected his cloak and left.

******

And so began their silent war!!!

Emilia before him, was spiraling out of control. He feared if she kept this charade up, eventually he would lose her. That was not an option. With every waking day it was something different and more daring she attempted and he didn't like it one bit. She went to every social gathering offered. He attended an evening soiree at Roxburg estate, though it was not as grand as the last it was still a huge affair. Familiar faces swarmed before him as he entered and spoke to few acquaintances and smiled. He was fully aware of the hand that squeezed his arms as he looked down at the red headed beauty accompanying him. He agreed to escort Viscount Chambers's cousin Charlotte to the soiree. She was a very beautiful young woman visiting from out of town. As a good favor to a friend, he agreed under the condition that she did not get her hopes on a romantic dalliance. They entered the ballroom and walked in unison greeting those that came forward to chat with them.

Emilia stood in the crowded circle of her friends as they whispered and giggled with gossip. She watched as another familiar face came into view with wide eyes and whispered.

"Did you see who entered with Lord McAllister." The feminine voice asked. They followed her eyes as they all gathered and turned to look in the direction she was pointing.

"Do you think that is his new lady?" one timidly asked.

Immediately Emilia looked at him, then at the woman next to him. An odd feeling grew in her stomach at the sight of him with another.

"No way she does not look his type," the venomous denial from another girl spoke up.

"Oh, do shut up, Lucille. And I suppose you know his type." The third female asked.

"What do you think, Emilia? They all looked her way and immediately she looked up to each of them, then looked at Dominic. She watched as he walked down the stairs and let the young woman by his side leave to join some other girls in a group. Tall, dark and gorgeous his gaze scanned the crowd.

Her heart slammed against her chest as their gazes locked.

Averting her eyes, she looked directly at the girl that asked the question before looking back into Dominics eyes. A devilish look of triumph twinkled in his eyes.

"Maybe she is one of his many lovers," She shrugged.

Deep down her stomach lurched at the thought and her eyes looked away. Just as fast she brushed off the feeling and turned to stare at the girls. Shortly they were surrounded by a group of young men vying for their attention.

*****

He stood and watched Emilia in deep conversation with her friends. The group of girls all stopped to look in his direction as he descended the steps with Charlotte on his arm. Their eyes met and immediately she looked away. His heart thundered behind his ribs at the sight of her. She was beautiful. Never had a woman looked so desirable to him. He was rooted to the spot captivated beyond reason, when the sound of her laughter danced along the music in the room from her lips to his ears. The young man by her side whispered to her, his anger began to rise as he watched the man that was enthralled with her, gently glide his finger down her arm.

He sat in a nearby corner and watched her under hooded eyes. He looked at the clock and moaned noticing that it was nine o'clock. He felt as if time was mocking him and decided to go even slower to goad him. He rubbed his temple that still throbbed from all the whiskey he drank last night. He tried with little effort to drown the thoughts of her, and drink himself senseless, but it didn't work. He woke up with her on his thoughts during the day and fantasized about bedding her by night.

He was beyond redemption.

He was beyond the fires of hell at this point.

"Brandy, my brother?" Dmitri drawled.

The tinge of the effects of Brandy was already evident in his friend slightly slurred speech.

Dominic looked at the amber liquid that invitingly swirled in the glass before him. Dimitri, his childhood friend had a drink in hand as always, pulled up a chair and joined him.

"So tell me brother, which one of the pretty fillys has caught your attention?"

Dominic shook his head, knowing this is not the time or the place to speak of his feelings for Emilia.

"Unfortunately, the object of my affections is not in sight," Dominic took swig brandy.

Liar, your object of your affection is right infront of you being pawed up by that heathen.

Dimitri laughed, giving him a pat on the shoulder. "Lady Hannah has you this gloom, eh?"

Dominic nodded with a half smile not wanting to admit to such a lie, but for the sake of not giving in to the urge of correcting his friend, he stayed quiet.

"I see Young Thomas has landed a nice companion for the night." He said, nodding in Emilia's direction.

"If he is anything like his father, the poor thing will have no chance of escaping him tonight."

Dominic frowned. "What do you mean?"

Dimitri sighed dramatically.

"It chills me to think he is the offspring of the man who has bedded a good handful of the women in this room."

Dominic's heart tightened at the thought.

"He is most eager the bloke, because he is trying to muddle her senses with wine," Dimitri smirked shaking his head.

Dominic turned to look at them. His heart raced with the way she candidly accepted a drink of wine from his glass. The act was sensual damn near bordering sexy. Dominic, seeing this, felt a surge of rage that he had the idea to just walk over to her and drag her away by force. He was livid.

As Charlotte sat beside them cutting their conversation short, his eyes averted to watch Emilia being pulled to the dance floor. The long conversation caught him off guard for the brief minutes that they spoke. He turned once more to scan the room to look for Emila.

She was gone.

*****

Emilia tried convincing herself to enjoy her evening as best she could. There was nothing she could change or do with respects to her feelings towards Dominic. He was someone she could not have.

Thomas Gordon- Lord Hayworth's - youngest son, was one of the many young men who had flocked to her side as soon as she entered the ballroom. He was handsome, and very coquettish. They danced most of the evening and talked. She slightly forgot that Dominic was staring at her. She glanced his way and noticed he spoke with an equally handsome blond Adonis. A scowl darkened his face with their conversation, he looked directly at her and she looked away.

At this point unbeknownst to the rest, she was on her fourth glass of wine. She nervously had snuck a couple in a swift swallow when she took a brief escape to the powder room. She looked down at the red sweet liquid and took another sip of it from Thomas's glass. The euphoric sensation of the wine just began to melt her senses and was getting stronger. Emilia laughed and flirted shamelessly with him appearing the least bit worried of the glaring stare of Dominic. She smiled up at Thomas when they finally slowed their pace when the music stopped.

"Thomas, I am feeling a bit faint. Let's go for a stroll in the garden for some fresh air." She murmured sweetly.

He grinned with a gorgeous twinkle in his eyes, he nodded and then they walked off towards the garden.

He led her out though the large French doors. They greeted others who were standing out in the dark night, taking in the beautiful star-lit night. They strolled for a while deeper into the garden. The effects of the wine engulfed her senses taking the edge off her awareness that he was leading her further away deeper into a secluded area of the garden.

"I have to say, I am most definitely enjoying the soiree." She smiled up at him.

They stopped briefly looking up at the sky. The darkness gave little view of his face, but she could tell he looked down at her. She began to sway a little. He chuckled and held her close, and immediately she knew what he was about. The plain thought of how he held her brought an alarming feeling to her that it was not right. She nervously looked around and saw they were further from the party. She regretted drinking so much wine because she could not shake the unusual feeling it gave her.

"As am I," He responded, pulling her closer. The feeling of being held so close made her uneasy. He was tall and a bit stronger than her, his intentions were evident. A bit worried she looked down and tried to pull away, but his grip tightened.

"I think it is better that we head back." Her voice trembled.

"Shh, don't worry, no one will notice we are gone." He murmured leaning closer.

"Thomas, please don't." she begged. She was afraid. This was not what she wanted at all. She tried to pull away, but his hold was tight she could feel his warmth... and..his unmistakable erection.

"Ill scream, if you don't let me go." She whimpered.

She began to shake as he pulled her close.

"Scream all you want, no one will hear you," He laughed sardonically.

His lips closed above hers.

She pushed and shoved at his shoulders and screamed loud enough only to be drowned out by his harsh kiss.

*****

He stood excusing himself, leaving Charlotte in Dimitri's company. Where the hell did she go? He scanned the room, but did not see her. With each passing moment his anger increased. Slowly he began walking around searching for her. A feeling persuaded him to walk out the French doors into the garden. He trailed the darkness further down listening for some telltale sign she was out here. He heard a muffled scream. His heart raced at the sound.

He immediately walked over to where the noise came from and froze where he stood. Emilia was struggling and pushing at Thomas's shoulder as he bent her back and forced a kiss on her. She pushed away in time to deliver a hard slap across his face. She stood bracing herself for the impact of his anger that never came. With a deathly growl Dominic caught Thomas's raised hand before he could hit her back, swirled him around and slammed his fist into his face. Pulling a dazed and confused Thomas up by the neck, he pulled him close. He felt as if he wanted to kill him. Shaking him and holding him at arms length he slammed his fist again into his stomach and yelled at him.

"Get the bloody hell out of here before I kill you," He snarled at Thomas, who at this point stumbled to the ground, stood and began to run.

Anger coursed through his veins. Fierce eyes looked in her direction.

She stood silently looking at him now. She trembled at the sight of him. Although she couldn't see Dominic's face clearly she knew he was angry.

"Dominic?" Her voice was shaking, she couldn't control the fright she was feeling.

"Did he hurt you?" he rasped.

"No" He heard the fright in her voice and he swore furiously. His anger terrified her.

"What the hell were you thinking, Emilia?" He croaked.

He turned to look at her. She stood silent in the darkness, thankful for the way it hid her face and his eye..

"Was the need so great, that you had to sneak off into the night with a man, Emilia? His icy tone told her of his anger.

Shocked at his accusation she was lost for words.

He reached for her arm and pulled her close.

"Answer me, you wanted him the way you wanted me." He hissed.

She stiffened at his word.

"No, that's not true," She pulled out of his grasp.

He laughed. The sound sent a chill up her spine. The powerful length of his body towered over her.

"Your shameless wanton actions this evening say's otherwise." He growled harshly.

Emilia drew back her hand and slapped him full across the face.

"I hate you!" she cried out.

He was fast. In an instant he had her in a tight grip, instinctively she let out a scream that he muffled with his mouth.

Her frantic struggles had no effect on him except it made him tighten his grip more. Never in her wildest dreams she imagined he could get this angry.

Before she knew what he was doing. She was laid forcibly to the lush grass beneath her. His hands captured her flailing arms and pinned them above her head. She was trapped and practically immobile. He stilled her cries with his mouth. He kissed her with a fierce need that was harsh and demanding.

"Is this what you wanted?" he whispered savagely against her lips before claiming them again.

The mixture of brandy and wine on their lips only intensified his desire.

His hands warm and strong caressed and exposed her breast, then slid beneath her dress to her thighs as he lay above her. The heaviness of his weight between her thighs sent a riveting sensation through her. Her heart thrummed in her chest with this new frightening feeling. His erection pressed into her and she whimpered desperately pushing at him. Fully aware of the feeling between her thighs and how in a matter of seconds the thin barrier that kept him from penetrating her could be easily be removed, she stopped her struggles.

Her voice quivered with a plea to let her go. Followed by a threat to scream if he didn't . He reared his head back to look down at her. He frightened her.

"Do it, and I will make damn sure I compromise you right here," She flinched at his threat. He meant every word.

"After all is that not what you wanted," he harshly whispered near her lips.

His harsh kisses continued until her struggling ceased and she lay beneath him shivering and crying. He lifted his head to look down at her.

She tremble with fear and her body shook with her sobs. Her dress hitched up to her waist and her breasts exposed. He did this. His anger drove him to do this to her. He had no right to do this.

You damn fool!

With a curse he shoved off of her on to his knees and looked down at her.

Immediately she covered her breasts and lowered her dress. Gently he scooped her trembling body up and lifted her into his arms.

"Listen to me, Emilia," he whispered, his arms tightened around her as she buried her face into his shoulder muffling her sobs.

"You're damn lucky I found you," He breathed harshly into her ear.

" Your reckless game you played could have ended far worse."

He walked with her still cradled against him towards the side of the estate unnoticed. Nodding to Clint his footman without question he opened the carriage door and Dominic climbed right in with Emilia in his arms. The door closed and the carriage moved out. Inside the cozy warmth and darkness that covered them, he cradled her across his lap and pulled her closer in his embrace. He did not mean for things to turn out this way. None of this was meant to happen. He was so enraged with what she was doing, he wanted to punish her. For what? He hadn't a clue. Her featherweight body lay still and unmoving. He tilted her chin up. She was passed out in his arms. He moved her hair from her face and caressed her cheeks. He gently placed a kiss on her lips and held her tightly.

"Forgive me." He whispered.

He leaned his head back and shut his eyes. This night was the worst of all. He breathed.

The carriage halted and when Clint opened the door , Dominic stepped out with Emilia still cradled in his arms. He walked slowly up to the entrance door that slowly swung open. Silently Jeoffrey came into view and met Dominic's sad stare.

"Take her," he spoke with the lump that was forming in his throat.

Because if not I will and I won't return her.

Without hesitation he placed her in Jeoffreys arms and watched as she buried her face into his shoulder.

He finally turned and walked off, disappeared into his carriage and left. Where he went to go home to get very, very drunk.

Bufford watched impatiently as Dominic began loosing all sense of sanity when it came to Emilia. It wouldn't be long before either he drinks himself to death or the husband of one of his mistresses shoots him dead. It was visible he was suffering for Emilia. He was being stubborn as an ox. Instead of courting her and doing the right thing, he was letting Emilia slip through his fingers.

He was going to have to take matters into his own hands and right this mess.

Tonight was one of the many nights after what transpired between Emilia and Dominic, that he drank himself into a stupor and passed out. Bufford sadly removed his shoes and left him where he was and walked to the kitchen to attend to his guests.

Glooming eyes watched each other over tea.

"Well, speak up! What do you suggest?" Sara impatiently waited for Bufford to talk.

"I say we push them together," He shrugged.

"That barbaric cur of your lord has surely hurt my mistress," Gertrude added.

"Your mistress needs to cool her temper and her willful ways," He retorted.

"Enough, all of you!" They all turned and stared at a straight faced Jeoffrey.

"Well, I say we dangle her before him and make her hard to get," Gertrude scrunched her nose.

"She is not a mouse Gertrude," Sarah scowled.

Considering the idea, Bufford clarified the thought.

"We all know and have seen it before. Why not help our petite wallflower turn into a budding exotic flower."

Worried gazes looked at one another.

"Turn our sweet mistress into a harlot is what you're saying old man?" Gertrude gave an offended gasp.

"No, Gertrude we turn her into an irresistible temptress that will eventually snare him," Sarah smiled impishly.

"I do say by the time we are done with those two all of the ton will surely suffer an apoplexy," Jeoffrey added nonchalantly sipping his tea.

With a mischievous smile, Bufford nodded.

"Why not tousle up the air a little around here and ruffle a few haughty feathers in the process," He gave a scheming smile.

"I fear we will all surely burn in the fires of hell for this," Gertrude nervously crossed herself.

"Lass, I am living in hell with that mans infernal behavior. I am surprised that half the women can walk straight in this town."

They gasped averting their eyes in shame.

"Then it is agreed?" Jeoffrey began to pass slices of apple pie to them.

"Yes, and we must act fast. I grow weary with the whores and wantons passing before me?" Bufford chucked a piece of apple pie furiously in his mouth.

Chapter 13

Some days had passed and she avoided him as much as she could. But it was inevitable because he was everywhere. According to Sarah and Gertrude they had a solution. Emilia sat stunned listening to the torrid stories and secrets of men and women in the boudoir from her two maids who surely and most definitely had too much time on their hands.

"Oh!very easy for you to say Gertrude, just toss my inhibition out the window."Emilia eyed her two scheming maids.

"Ye, something like that. Throw all your seductive wiles at him, milady." They both took turns talking.

"But, without giving it up," Gertrude eyed Sarah with a warning glare before elbowing her.

She sat in horror of the idea.

Yes, she was young, but to act in such a fashion. Could she do it? She went back to how when she saw Lady Hannah and how she acted in bed with him. A little embarrassed about being so bold made her nervous. Then again, he wants a woman experienced and daring.

"Alright, I will do it. It's about time the good girl becomes a little naughty," She tilted up a defiant stare. Sounding more unsure than anything she jumped at their squeals as they pulled her into a group hug.

Over the course of the week, they had her busy, very busy. Between Gertrude, Sarah and Bufford her face flamed red and grew hot with shame and embarrassment over their conversations of flirting, seduction, sex and lust.

Flustered with so much information she feared she would put the town whore to shame.

Her eyes bulged.

"Can I really do that? But, that is so wrong and...surely forbidden," She flushed at Sarah's broad sinful grin.

"Oh yes, milady and he will surely be looking for you after that."

Right then Gertrude appeared before them and knelt in front of Emilia brandishing a beautiful jeweled dagger in its sheath. Lifting it to the light, she watched it sparkle. Swallowing, she nervously breathed.

"And what do you pretend I do with this...Stab him...?"She asked incredulously.

Shifting in her seat, Sarah cleared her throat.

"That may very well keep your virtue intact. Because after a couple of days of this dangerous game, it will most likely be in peril."

With that news, Emilia shot upright out of her chair.

"I can't do this; all of you have gone daft," She paced in a panic.

"Do you love him?" Gertrude questioned pulling Emilia to face her with a stern glare.

"Yes, with all of my heart," She answered with an ardent breath.

"Then fight for it," Gertrude shoved the dagger in her hand.

*****

That evening they all went for a walk in the park where she sat with Bufford and they talked.

"It will work, you know," he said.

Looking at him quietly, "How can you be so sure, Bufford? " She asked with trepidation in her voice.

"The way he stares at you, and when he speaks of you his eyes light up."

She silently listened to him.

"He is slowly getting tired of Lady Hannah's visits," he mentioned triumphantly.

"And I think it's time you paid him those visits." He shot her a suggestive smile.

She sat surprised and silent.

"Tomorrow night will be perfect." He looked straight ahead.

She shot him an astonished gaze, "T..tomorrow night?" she sat nervously looking at him.

"Tomorrow night, The Earl of Cromwell and his wife will be hosting a masquerade ball; one Dominic will attend for a short while," he informed her.

She silently listened.

She did not look too convinced.

"Emilia, deep within you there is a wild Scottish rose that needs to take root on what's going on out here. The petite wallflower needs to blossom into that rose." He told her ardently.

"How is that ol' man Ferguson." He gave a Scottish lilt to his speech and shot a side gaze.

"You know my grandfather." She beamed in surprise.

"And your mother, may she rest in peace." He looked up.

He never went into detail, but acknowledged that years ago they lived here.

Their conversation ended, and she sat for a while, taking in all what was learned and what was at stake. She would lose him being married to another. On the other hand, she would lose him to the grasp of another woman. And, she wanted neither to happen. Her heart was already lost to him. So what else did she have to lose?

Pretty much your innocence, because after this you don't stand a chance of keeping it safe.

*****

He wearily got dressed in his attire. He thought repeatedly should he go? Although, the invitation did say everyone was to wear masks. It was a night where no one knew who you were. He would be able to hide who he was. Either way the idea still did not peak his interest. What he really wanted to know is if Emilia would attend. Knowing her uncle, he would probably force her to attend to get her out to mingle with potential suitors.

He could not get his mind off of her or the fire in her gaze when they argued for the first time.. Letting out a deep breath, she was doing a number on him.

With a soft knock on the door, he bid Bufford to enter.

"Your carriage awaits, M'lord."

Nodding, he turned to leave.

He stepped into the waiting carriage.

He sat back and watched the buildings pass in a blur.

Minutes later, the carriage pulled up to the posh estates of the Earl.

Carriages one by one pulled up. Familiar faces came into view. He plied on the fake smile and greeted those entering with him.

Lush fabrics and lights lined the ballroom.

Wine and champagne were served. Masks were on very few faces. Music and dancing began. His eyes searched the crowd for her. The young girls who lined the opposite wall did not fit her description. He knew her too well, well at least; he thought he did.

The dance lulled in his eyes forever. He quickly looked at the large clock. A little disappointed and bored, he turned towards the entrance door. Trying to avoid the lust filled stares of the incoming female guests. He quickly entered his carriage and left.

Standing before the speculating gaze, she nervously bit her lip. "You look gorgeous" Bufford held Emilia at arm's length.

She had to build up her courage. Tonight, would be the night of his undoing.

She stood before the large mirror in his bedroom, the beautiful girl who stared back at her was a stranger to her. The flirtatious bodice and sequined dress accented her curves. Slowly, she placed the matching mask with elaborate feathers above her eyes. She sat in the dark corner of his room in a large leather chair waiting.

His carriage arrived just as Bufford told her he would.

She had to remain strong, enticing and cunning there was no room for error.

*****

He entered his room and shut the door behind him. She watched him for a while as he leaned against the door and began removing his waistcoat and his cravat.

He caught the silhouette of a figure sitting in the dark corner of the room.

With a smile pulling at the side of his lips, he knew Hannah would be somewhere lurking around because she wasn't at the ball.

He continued to unbutton his shirt.

"Are you going to sit there all night or are you coming to bed?"

She gave no answer.

He stood staring at her in the chair.

Slowly, she stood and began walking leisurely towards him. His seductive smile turned puzzling. The woman had on a breathtaking gown. He noticed that the woman standing before him wasn't Hannah.

Who was she?

"Why, hello there!" He huskily greeted her.

She never answered back.

She slowly walked around him gliding her fingers down one arm, his back, his other arm then his chest. His lips curved at her exploration.

"May I at least have a name, milady." He asked.

Slowly, she shook her head no.

She reached down and held his hand and pulled him in the direction of his bed.

With a wicked smile, he followed.

She pushed him to sit down and crawled above him helping him scoot back until he was resting up against his pillows. She sat above him and planted her soft rump on his manhood, and he gave a moan.

He was loving this.

His hands gently touched her waist, but she placed them at his side. With a chuckle, he sat back agreeing to play her game. She was a mystery to him. It had to be someone he already knew. Which one of his sensual lady friends, would try something so...bold, daring and sexy?

Lady Amanda?

Countess Julianna?

He looked her up and down with such a gaze that her heart raced at the way his cock hardened beneath her.

He watched her reach into her bodice, between her very low neckline pulling out a long slim piece of cloth. She pulled his left hand up and tied it to the bedpost. Then she reached for his right and did the same. Tied really snug and his senses tingling with excitement he lay there before her, arms stretched out and vulnerable.

His heart roared in his ears watching her glide her finger over his chest.

He gasped when she ferociously ripped his shirt open the echo of the few buttons left bounced off the walls.

His seductive grin caught her shadowed eyes. "That, my sweet was my favorite shirt,"

She smiled, leaned forward and dipped her head towards his neck and kissed him. She sealed hot kisses down to his stomach. She loved the hold she had on him. Leaning forward again she kissed him again on his left cheek and worked her way up to his ear. Her tongue worked him to the brink that his toes began to curl in his Hessian boots.

Her scent peaked his interest because it was one he did not recognize and what drove him crazy.

His fast breathing felt so good against her ear. He moaned and groaned and begged her to let him loose.

She quieted his suffering with a sweet kiss. A kiss, she controlled. His moans and gasps came quicker as she ground her rump on his swollen cock.

He leaned his head back losing his self in the feel of her taking such liberties with him.

She stopped long enough to bring down her own frenzied pleasure to work on his.

She glided down his body and his eyes glistening with lust and fire when he felt her fingers tugging at the buttons to his breeches. The sound that came from his lips made her smile as she freed him. Warm fingers caressed and played with his jumping cock making it hard like stone.

Delicate warm fingers glided up and down slowly on his swollen shaft and twitched in her hand.

What came next was his undoing.

In the throes of a beginning climax, she leaned forward and kissed is mouth sucked his lips plunging her tongue into his mouth the way he did it to her. It was succulent, demanding and downright sexy.

She pulled away from his lips. His eyes focused on the juicy plumpness that had him on the brink of insanity.

Her eyes fixed on his, and he watched her smile and slowly reach for her mask.

She took it off.

The look on his face was amazing; his eyes went wide from surprised, to a wicked twinkle to a hot gaze.

His wide wicked grin promised her something dark and sinful.

Never in a million years would he imagine that this sweet yet meek lovely girl could turn into a gorgeous and tempting minx.

Now he really wanted her to untie him.

"Sweeting untie me" his voice was sexual and low.

Her eyes sparkled with mischief.

He cleared his throat only uncertain of her next move. Lord, he only wanted one hand free to touch her.

His heart quickened when she tucked her lower lip between her teeth. A sign of shyness and wanting that he loved when she did it. Her coyness was gone in a matter of seconds.

"Love, untie me" his stare hot and sultry turned demanding.

Her unnerving silence only peaked his anger a tinge.

His face in awe watched her when she straddled him and began pumping his cock with her hand, squeezing and stroking it with a torturing sensual motion at that moment she knew she was treading dangerous ground .His hips bucked. His eyes never left hers. Her other hand went beneath her dress. Under hood eyes, he watched her reach between her thighs and touch herself. She looked so bloody delicious he wanted to fuck her.

His blood rushed to his cock with each stroke. She continued to pleasure them both until fireworks went off and she whimpered with his groan and curses. His body shuddered and growled. Panting and weak she moved off him. She plopped to his side on her back trying to control her trembling body and the pounding between her legs. Still dazed in his release not able to touch or caress her was maddening. He watched her chest rise and fall quickly. Smiling to himself that she enjoyed herself just as much.

A while had passed.

"Emilia, untie me love."

Her heart quickened, just hearing his husky voice, brought tingling back between her thighs.

She stayed silent.

He sighed.

She slowly sat up and went to his side. Nervously she licked her lips, his hot gaze never leaving her face.

He watched her crawl closer to him. He was fascinated with her flushed look. Her hair hung in tossled soft curls around her face.

Now her hands shaking went to untie his hand, but the look in his eyes stilled her hand. His dangerous, hot and sexy glare promised something wicked for her behavior.

"Untie me, I promise I won't try anything." His gorgeous blue gems turned dark.

How she wanted to feel his hands all over her body.

She leaned into kiss him one last time. Pulling away, he chuckled wickedly.

"You're not going to untie me, are you?"

With a beautiful smile, she shook her head.

With a devilish grin, he stared at her with a gaze that set her heart into a patter.

"When I get a hold of you my sexy minx, I'm going to ride you so hard and good your legs are going to fall off." His glare was hot with promise.

She looked exquisite and sated with wild abandon, naughty and seductive. Like a lioness on the prowl, her green eyes twinkled at his words and she leaned closer to him, nose to nose she whispered near his lips.

"Is that a promise m'lord?" her voice sweet seductive and alluring.

"Indeed it is" he growled.

Before he could catch her lips with his, like a playful kitten waiting for him to join the play she climbed off him, turned and left him there. Closing the door behind her, she trembled leaning against the door. His laugh trailed after her. So sexy, seductive and wicked.

"Emilia when I get my hands on you...."

Leaning her head against the door, she let out a nervous breathless giggle.

With the help of her maids, she was whisked off in her carriage to go home.

He sat against the pillows, his eyes closed, his thoughts still swimming of her seductive play. He grinned before biting down on his lips marveling about the way she sexually enticed him. How in bloody hell did she get this seductive?

The slight tap on the door of the one guilty in this game came into view.

Silent and expressionless Bufford came into view.

The idea was good he thought, but the view of her handy work was brilliant. Bufford untied Dominic.

He calmly sat on the bed folded his hands before his manhood and crossed his legs. With a chilling smile, he regarded Bufford.

"Did you have anything to do with this, Bufford?" he asked.

Bufford's straight face looked at Dominic.

"I don't have a clue of what you are insinuating m'lord,"

With an amused chuckle, Dominic shook his head.

With that, Bufford turned walking with a smile on his face, he bid Dominic a good night.

He sat back and smiled at what unfolded tonight.

Chapter 14

S he lay awake, dazed at her boldness, her display of sheer audacity and she loved it. The gorgeous look on his face when she pulled off her mask.

How was she going to continue this, to what end?. How she wanted his manhood inside her with a sense of urgency. Slowly she glided her fingers in between her legs. Closing her eyes the image of him before her as she pleasured herself along with him was a sexual arousal she needed to calm. A warm heat crept up her cheeks, she glided a finger through her wet folds and rubbed her sensitive pearl until the room around her began to spin fast. A breath and pant escaped her as she muffled a scream of her climatic release into her pillow. Heart thumping and sated, she slowly floated down from the clouds and let sleep claim her.

*****

The morning light met her head on as she awoke refreshed and well rested. The slight tap on her door came and the familiar blonde head of Sarah popped into view. Sitting up she smiled giddy looking at her and bid her to enter. With a pat on her bed urging Sarah to sit she squealed with delight.Like two sisters sharing their secrets they giggled in hushed whispers until Gertrude entered the three sat and spoke of what transpired the night before. Tossed back on her back, she sighed closing her eyes.

"I am surely without redemption!" her heart pounded.

Slowly she placed her hands above her beating heart that was beating so fast she was shaking.

"He is the love of my life." She smiled.

*****

Some days had passed. After what she did, It was agreed that she needed to avoid him at all costs. It was time to wait and see just exactly how the Marquess will play. She stayed extra busy and occupied with Luncheons, games and tea parties.

She sat with her aunt at Lady Sophia's piquet party, While their husbands sat in the study, the women drank tea in the garden. They all sat around and played ever so often a gossip here and a gossip there. Her ears opened further when they spoke of Dominic and how we went to the ball but didn't stay long.

"It was as if he were there searching for someone." Lady Bethanny said.

An impish wrinkle of another woman chimed in.

"Who do you think he could have been looking for.?" another one asked.

If you only knew, it was me who he searched for.

Heat crept up her cheeks at the thought of knowing how she had him that night.

Since the ton gossiped mercifully, he was able to locate where his little minx was. Lady Sophia had a small gathering of ladies over all of which included the presence of Emilia. He sat back in the cool shade scheming and planning.

No doubt at the same time Lord Humphry was there as well with friends playing cards.

He was greeted by the butler and announced with Lord Humprhy who gladly invited him in to their little clandestine gambling, unbeknownst to his wife of course. He was ushered in quickly where the rest of familiar faces greeted him, handed him a cigar and a fine glass of brandy. Exactly what he needed.

He sat opposite the window that gave a clear view of the garden and its inhabitants.

He coolly played his game like a champ while observing under hooded eyes the gorgeous object of his affection.

The game drolled on for a moment, the men became more rambunctious with hearty laughs due to playful banter all the while he grazed his vision over to the window.

*****

The opportunity presented itself and he watched her stand and leave the group of ladies no doubt to escape. At that moment, he cleared his throat and excused himself for a brief moment.

He went in search to see where she went. He turned the hall just in time to see her skirt dissappear into a refreshing room. Looking both ways, he walked quickly to the door.

She stood near the basin on the table filled with water and rose petals, white cloths were folded of to the side she grabbed one and dipped it into the water. Bringing the moist cloth to her nose she inhaled the scented water and began to wipe her face and neck. She never heard the soft click of the door or the sexual gaze of Dominic behind her.

The soft click of the door made her turn to see who entered.

She turned around and froze in place.

The look in her eyes brought a seductive grin to his lips that made her legs weak.

"Have you been avoiding me, love?" his voice husky and honeyed that her stomach dipped and throbbing began between her thighs.

Her heart pummeled in her chest with his hungry gaze and gorgeous eyes that swept over her from head to toe.

She wasn't prepared for this encounter at all. It's funny how her two maids failed to mention this part of the plan.

What to do when you're trapped by a Marquess on the prowl.

He straightened away from the door very slowly. His gaze hypnotically held her in place.

He stood before her. She slowly looked up and held his gaze, the sheer shiver of excitement had her heart racing like hell in her chest. At that moment, it dawned on her that she was seriously in his grasp and completely in trouble.

He was all muscles before her and absolutely gorgeous.

Gently he raised his fingers to caress her cheek. She trembled with his touch.

"You have no idea what you started do you?" he grinned with a twinkle in his eyes.

Quickly she licked her lips, and held his gaze and his smile. Oh! His smile.

"Well let me enlighten you, my sweet vixen," His voice was soft.

He caressed her neck and pulled her softly into a kiss.

The provocative play of his tongue with hers just completely undid her train of thought. The warmth of his body was playing havoc with her senses.

He could not get enough of her the need for her was too great.

He walked with her and leaned her up against the table.

"I want to show what the consequences are for your naughty actions," He whispered.

His voice like sweet honey caressed her lips.

He leaned her against the table, slowly pulling up her skirts. He rubbed his protruding cock through his breeches on the fabric that hid her wet folds. She whimpered when he touched her.

Dominic dipped his head and kiss her neck. His warm hand pulled her bodice down and freed her breasts. He kissed each soft globe before taking the hardening nipple into his mouth. Heat crept up her cheek and her breathing increased. Through hot kisses and heavy breathing, he undid his breeches to free his cock. He just had to touch her with it and rub it against her wetness. The need to bury it deep inside her had him clawing for self control. They both knew he could not and must not penetrate her, but her virtue hung in the balance at this point ......

and she didn't care.

All she wanted was for him to sink his erection in her so bad that her insides began to hurt. He rubbed and lathered it with her wetness and groaned at the feel of her.

She broke away from his kiss and begged him in a whimpering plea to fuck her.

Shaking his head breathlessly, he whispered in a devilish smile.

"We can't give in so easy love, this game has just begun,"

He sat her on the edge of the table. He wasn't going to ravish her like he would like to, but, she wasn't leaving this room without getting pleasured.

Her eyes glazed over with lust, watched as he knelt before her, he spread her legs and his lips kissed her....there. He stared up at her with the hungriest gaze that just made her tremor. She watched as his lips close over her intimate part, sucked and licked her until the room began to spin before her eyes and got extremely hot. She gasped with each kiss and plunge of his tongue. He laid claim to his prize.

Yes his.

He sucked and caressed her, his hand on her rump kneading and squeezing it. Her hips began to move with the rhythm of his tongue. He watched her shudder before him, a devilish smile splayed on his lips, watching her breathe hard, her face flush and trying to control herself. The look of her slender throat and her breasts as they quivered with here breathing, deepened his tongue between her folds. Her fingers wove through his hair. When he saw her reaching the peak of her climax, he slowly stood leaving her on the edge. Breathing hard and still wanting more she stared into his eyes. His gorgeous blue eyes twinkled with satisfaction and wickedness.

Payback!

She gasped when she understood with clarity what he was doing, then his smile widened.

He watched her eyes turn a dark shade of green and it made her look so wild and beautiful. He leaned closer as to give her a kiss only to place his lingering kiss on her neck.

His hand caressed her cheek.

"I want to savor the taste of you on my lips," He sensually tasted his lips with his tongue.

With a gasp she closed her eyes to the need of him between her thighs and aching for her release that never came.

"And, I believe we are even, my love."

She watched him turn towards the door and before he left, he gave her the most sexiest wink and left her hot, wet and on shaky legs. She realized at that moment it would be the beginning of her most erotic endeavor and she was ready.

*****

Their sexy cat and mouse game with one another was an arousing sexual excitement that left them looking for more. He wanted her and she wanted him.

Their brief glances at each other at social events were endearing and coquettish. He cooly pretended to partake in frivolous talk, while glancing her way and catching her beautiful smile while listening to something funny. His heart was beating for her and she knew it. His gorgeous good looks were her undoing. When he comes into view all time stops for her.

By day, they were on the prowl for each other. One catching the other alone and by surprise. While by night, it was torture.

*****

He sat back and watched her under hooded eyes at a dinner party. She was playing very hard to get and dangling all her seductive wilds before him leaving his world in total upheaval. He had thought all along that what he felt for her was just affection, lust or infatuation. He was dead wrong.

He undeniably loved her.

She sat on the floor in their drawing room with her aunt doing the painful, boring task of stitching and sewing, if she pricked her finger one more time, she will be handing her aunt a blood stained hem. Her uncle sat in a nearby chair conversing with them when Jeffry entered with a letter.

An invitation to Lord & Lady Ruxford's Autumn Soiree.

Entertainment, Dinner and a chance to partake in political talks. She sat back and listened to the rest of the invitation. As the soiree was for adults only, she, to her relief could not attend. Her uncle regarded her.

"Emilia my child, you will stay home with Gertrude and Sarah while your aunt and I attend". Answering her uncle with a polite, mature tone brought a smile to his face.

"Very well then, I guess we will be attending." he piped out smiling at her aunt.

She continued her stitching with a smile. Finally an event she could not attend she never liked crowded social events or the unnecessary attention she received.

A bit gloom for one part it would be one event she could not attend, but Dominic could and there is no doubt Lady Hannah would be there ogling him.

She shrugged off the notion there was nothing she could do but wait to run into him later she smiled to herself.

Dominic sat back and smiled reading the invitation. His eyes arched at the wordings for adults only. He concluded that Emilia wouldn't attend. A surge of happiness and longing went through him. A week had passed by he had only had glimpses of her and smiles his way to hold him but it wasn't enough.

The Soiree was to start at six and would last into the wee hours in the morning. He waited for a while before leaving.

*****

Exhausted she stretched out in bed. She stared at the canopied ceiling for a while drowsiness danced on her lids.

Two pairs of eyes watched the beguiling blue eyes of their visitor with crossed arms against the door jam.

"M'lord but ..." Gertrude stammered.

"Sooner or later, we are bound to run in to eachother, ladies," he smiled.

"Leave them be Gertrude, don't you see he wants to be with her." Sarah argued.

Hesitating, she looked skeptically at him, then gave him a warning glare.

"Don't get caught."

With a graceful coquettish bow, he rendered them with senseless giggles. With that he took two stairs at a time and walked quietly to her door. He paused, not knowing what to do. Slowly he pulled the handle of the lock and pushed it open.

A lamp with little glowing light sat on a nearby table gave enough for him to see her sleeping form on the bed.

He neared a chair in the corner and took off his overcoat, waistcoat, cravat, and his boots. He padded slowly over to her bed and looked down at her. Her hair fanned out around her. One leg hung exposed. A bare shoulder from her chemise was showing. She was beautiful. He gently climbed above her, leaned in and kissed her like the sleeping beauty she is.

Her eyes opened slowly and she sweetly caressed his cheek and kissed him back.

"I had to see you," he nuzzled his face into the warmth of her neck.

They caressed each other slowly and kissed so passionately as if it would be their last night together. Her nearness just made his heart clamor hard in his chest.

He leaned to his side and looked down at her, their legs intertwined; she traced her fingers along his jaw and lips. For a while, he stared into those eyes.

"Am I dreaming m'lord? " She asked, still foggy with sleep.

He smiled and shook his head.

"If you are then so am I." he replied with a gorgeous grin.

They spoke for a while and kissed. He loved being in her company.

"Dominic." she lowered her gaze.

He silently waited for her to speak.

"I wish we were back at Grisham" She looked into his eyes.

"As do I, " he replied softly.

He watched her nervously fold her bottom lip between her teeth.

"I wish we could have the closeness we had before I.....ruined it." Her eyes began to pool with tears.

His eyes softened and his stare grew hard.

"You did not ruin anything, that night I could not contain myself. From the moment I laid my eyes upon you, I wanted you." He leaned closer and caressed her cheek.

She kissed him.

"I did to. I had this feeling we were destined to be together." She smiled.

Her gaze held his.

"I want.... to feel your body next to mine, your warmth."

She slowly reached up and unbuttoned his shirt, they sat up together and slowly piece by piece removed every inch of their clothing all barriers were gone.

Kneeling close together, he glanced over the site of her.

A budding beauty.

She kissed his neck, his chest, his shoulders until he caressed her and did the same. It was a sensual exploration that they marveled in.

Her heart quickened with the touch of his strong hands.

Her inner thighs became wet with his caress and kisses, her breath hot on his skin hardened his cock.

His mind rolled with images of this night. This time it was playing before him vividly. If he went any further, there was no turning back.

Their eyes met again and stayed locked on one another.

He laid her down slowly against her pillows. The warmth of his skin, the closeness of his muscular body sent waves of pleasure through her. His lips slowly joined hers for a kiss that spoke volumes of the love they felt for one another.

Her breathing was heavy and she was trembling with desire.

"Are you sure this is what you want?" He breathed into her lips before kissing them again.

She shook her head.

"There is no turning back, Emilia." He croaked.

"I want this more than anything, I want you and no other. I Love you, Dominic."

Her eyes held tears. The overwhelming urge in him to love and devour her was too much.

"I love you more." He whispered.

He braced himself between her thighs carefully. He pressed his swollen manhood to her softness, looking into eyes that looked back at him with so much love and trust. She lovingly pulled him close for a kiss drowning out her whimper as he pushed slowly and as gently as he could into her tearing her maidenhead. She was so tight and warm around him,he groaned , buried his face in her neck and stood still. Wracked with heavy breathing, she clung to him, he filled her to the rim and she began to shudder.

He slowly raised his head and looked into her eyes, he caressed her cheek.

"Relax for me, my love," he whispered breathlessly.

With that said, he began to move slowly thrusting into her with a softness and a care while he lovingly kissed her. He wanted to make it slow and enjoy the feeling of her. Make sweet love to her like his life depended on it. Strong warm hands rubbed and caressed her thighs. She rubbed his back and buttocks reveling in the feel of his muscles flexing with each thrust. They moved together in unison with such passion that friction was working them both. Each thrust was emphasized with a sensual motion of his hips, she couldn't contain herself. A mixture of heat and pleasure was building between them nearing a climax so great she dug her nails into him that he cursed closing his lips on hers, he thrust harder with a fierce desire.

She writhed beneath him, arching her back, giving him a glorious view of her breasts. He cried out her name and she came for him. Her insides clenched around him so tight they both shuttered with ecstasy at last.

Spent, exhausted and fully sated their bodies slowly began to descend from the skies. Her skin still tingling from his lovemaking still made her tremble with desire.

He pulled her close into his embrace, she felt so good by his side.

The feel of her arms and legs tangled in wild abandonment with his was an overwhelming feeling he wanted to feel forever.

Her head was cradled on his shoulder. The lovemaking tired them so much that she let the warmth of his body over take her senses until she fell asleep.

His sleep was light. He enjoyed the feel of her warm lithe body entwined with his. This was not mare frolicking in bed that they had.

He made love to her.

With hesitation, he slipped out in the wee hours of the morning. He had to leave quickly before he lost himself in her warm embrace and kisses. With plans to see her soon, he dressed and then left.

Chapter 15

He sat in his study eyeing his ledgers, not able to concentrate. He smiled because he was severely distracted by his thoughts of Emilia. The things she did to him were...breathtaking, lusty, damn near bordering erotic. Although they made love for the first time they continued their little cat and mouse game, Him being the mouse of course and her his lioness, he chuckled to himself. But the tables changed in his favor and the lion sought out his mate.

He closed his eyes reminiscing in their last encounter it was so hot his cock jumped at the vision of it in his head. He could not forget the look in those gorgeous green eyes when he surprised her at Lady Dabney's luncheon. He took advantage of his invitation, never doing so before he showed up. Oddly enough, he didn't see her, so he went in search for her. Admiring the view of her, He stood behind her in the study where he found her. She preferred the solitude and the comfort of being alone in a quiet place. When he checked his surroundings, he shut and locked the doors. Leaning against them, he watched her stiffen and slowly turn.

"Our last game of hide and seek left me.... Unsated." his low, seductive voice made her eyes twinkle.

Slowly stepping behind a chair, she rested her fingers on its backing and looked up at him with a teasing stare.

"Oh! Well, I distinctly remember m'lord the rules clearly stated that if you found me, you could have me." She bit her bottom lip enjoying her taunt.

Slowly he walked forward and stood before the chair. The sight of him was exquisite. An Adonis in his own right.

"I would like a rematch then." he grinned seductively.

Contemplating she stared at him cocking her head to the side as she looked him up and down then smiled.

"What does the winner get?" She bit her lips.

With a devilish grin, he looked down at her.

"Pleasure"

"And the loser." she added, licking her lips.

"Give in to the winner's wishes"

She smiled and looked away from his devilish smile.

Her cheeks turned a deep pink her eyes held his as he slowly walked around the chair and she moved carefully around the opposite side.

The chase was all the more exciting as their hearts raced with the thrill of a sexual encounter.

She darted quickly to his side, dodging him, but she wasn't quick enough. His muscular arm caught her by the waist and she gave in to his warm embrace. His heavily breathing near her lips, he claimed victory. He kissed her so passionately she let out such sweet moan. He kissed her neck and the skin near her breasts.

He whispered in her ears, hot and ready for her.

"I can't wait to get you alone; we can't take our chances of getting caught here." he growled.

She broke away the kiss and looked up at him.

In her eyes, he saw she had other plans. With fluid motion, she undid his cock from his breeches turned him towards the chair sat him down, straddled him and glided it into her.

"Sweet Mercy!!!" He cursed.

She covered her lips with his and provocatively sucked and kissed his lips. She began grinding her waist and her rump onto his erection until the tightness, friction and warmth had him swearing. He grabbed her waist and guided her up and down slowly. His release came like barrels of hot water over him. He groaned out loud and she covered his mouth with her hand and mischievously put her finger to her lips and gave one last grind before he spilled his seed in her. Her throbbing and tightness made him shudder. With a shaky breathless chuckle, he pulled her close for a kiss.

"Minx!" he grinned.

The game just got interesting.

She wrinkled her nose and stuck out her tongue teasingly, kissed him then quickly left.

*****

The slight knock on the door broke his thoughts. He bid Bufford to enter.

"M'lord Dimitri is here for a visit."

With a nod, he waited for his friend to enter.

The smile of his old friend came into view. With a hearty laugh, he grabbed his friend in a bear hug.

Holding him out at arm's length, he grinned.

"Congratulations, my friend, I see the newlywed life has done you good, look at you, " he pat him on the back with another hug before showing him to a nearby seat.

"You my friend, are looking mighty rested, I see a light in you I have never seen before," Dimitri leaned back and looked at Dominic with a grin.

With a laugh, Dominic looked away grinning not able to contain his own joy.

"Tell me brother, hold nothing back," Dimitri with an interested glare waited for Dominic to talk.

With a smile and a sigh, Dominic through his head back looking up at the ceiling, he looked for the words to express what was the cause of so much joy.

"Brother, I don't know where to begin." Dominic chuckled

"Start from the beginning is it a woman?" Dimitri grinned.

Dominic smiled, nodding his head.

With wide eyes, Dimitri leaned forward.

"Lady Hannah finally widowed and you plan to marry."

Dominic scowled shaking his head.

"No, my brother I can assure you it is not lady Hannah that has me this way." He gave a wry smile with little emotion.

With raised eyebrows, he sat back and waited for Dominic to reveal his secret.

"I'm completely in love with a young beauty."

"Do you remember the young girl at The Wakefield Ball? Emilia Westham?" Dominic asked.

Dimitri nodded confused.

"How?... when...? Did you get close enough to meet her?" Dimitri sat forward now peaked with interest.

Dominic began from the beginning of his story to the present day. Dimitri sat back for a while in awe.

"You cheeky bastard!, When were you going to tell me all of this?" Dimitri in surprise smiled.

Dominic laughed, then he fell silent.

Concern grew in Dimitri's eyes.

"What is wrong?"

"I love her. And, I don't think I can bare the thought of losing her to another man." Dominic voice faltered on the last word.

"Then why don't you marry her?" Shaking his head Dominic stood and turned to the window.

"I can't, it is complicated, " He hesitated.

"Why is it complicated?" confused Dimitri looked at him.

"You know the scandalous life I live, the women, the drinking, the gambling. I am not a good match. The sordid life I lived will pose a problem for her,"

"Dominic what does that have to do with marrying the woman you love?"

"Come now Dimitri! you know with a union like ours, they will surely chew her up and spit her out with gossip and scandal. I can't put her through that. You know how harsh the ton is." He angrily replied.

"Besides, she needs a good husband. Someone with good standing and an unmarked past, scandal free." the bittersweet reality fell from his lips and he hated the truth that wrung from it.

"Oh, Posh!, since when do you care what the ton says. So, you would prefer to let a crotchety old man take her for his wife?"

Silently, he listened to Dimitri. His friend was right.

They talked freely about everything.

Chapter 16

She sat nervously listening to the gossip, the torrid love affairs gone awry, the divorce of one couple, the lovers passed thru this and that person. One newly heard was Lady Hannah's husband the Duke was ill, perhaps on his deathbed. Secretly she prayed it was not so because if it was she would no doubt want to sink her paws into Dominic. She looked down at herself. She was nothing like her. She was voluptuous, beautiful, with class and prestige. In truth, she was holding onto something that was impossible, she would never be Dominic's wife. So, why keep him from her?

Night had fallen and like some or other nights, he would sneak in to be with her. They lay awake whispering about each other's day. A slipped giggle and chuckle would be hushed with a kiss, like children they slid beneath the covers and continued their chatter in hushed voices.

The warm fire crackled and the low light from the fire gave the room a soft glow.

Content they lay facing one another.

After a while, she looked away from his eyes and turned on her back. Shortly he moved on his elbow and looked down at her.

"What is wrong?"

She looked into his eyes.

"I heard that Lady Hannah's husband is ill and possibly may die." her voice was low, but he could hear the worry in it.

He stayed silent for a while looking down at her.

"If that happens, she will come looking for you." She murmured softly.

"And what makes you think I would have her." He chuckled.

She lowered her eyes.

"You two have a past. Besides, she is.. Very beautiful and wealthy." she sadly averted her gaze.

He gently caressed her cheek, bringing her eyes to his.

"We have a past, Emilia and that is all it is. A past, I don't love her, I love you. No riches in the world would ever change that. And as far as beauty goes, you by far my love are more beautiful."

"Yes, but...."

As stubborn as he knew her to be, he rolled his eyes mockingly and buried his face in her neck and listened to her blurt out her worries and concerns until she was done.

Looking down at her, he smiled at her caressing her cheek with the back of his hand.

A little bothered that he wasn't taking her worries seriously, her brows furrowed. A look that he hadn't seen in so long, but on her it never marred her gorgeous eyes.

"You know you look enchanting when you get upset. Your eyes darken and your cheeks turn red." He teased.

"m'lord are you listening to me." she pouted.

With raised brows, he looked at her.

"So, we are back to formalities are we now?" he chuckled.

Silently she looked away from his teasing smile.

With a sigh, he pulled her closer and kissed her lips.

Lying above her, he cradled himself between her legs.

"How can I show you that you have nothing to worry about?" his voice husky and warm against her lips.

He kissed her again.

"You are the only one I love."

Her eyes filled with worry stared into his for reassurance; he glided her chemise up to her waist and smiled at her response to his touch. She was ready for him.

His cock hard with need slipped into her tight velvety wetness, the warmth just made him groan.

The sensual slow motion made her whimper. He took his slow time and made sweet love to her. He whispered, his love for her and proved it with each soft stroke.

"I want you to feel me inside of you, how much I need you, the things you do to me when you're close to me."

His hips with elaborate movements made her gasp arching her back.

He slowly worked her into a frenzy of desire.

He sucked on her lips and tongue as she did to him, she writhed beneath him matching his movements and he moaned more sweet words.

The peak of their climax had them panting with each caress of his warm hands on her thighs and rump. The feel of her hands caressing his back made his head spin.

She panted, her love for him, as he brought her over the edge.

He closed his lips over hers to muffle her and cry. Digging her nails into his back, he thrust deep, feeling her insides tighten around him more. Releasing his seed with a shudder and a wave of heat washed over them both as they went over the top.

Slowly they floated down breathless and weak.

Lying above her, he lifted his head to look down at her. Her long lashes fanned her cheeks, he kissed her nose. Slowly her eyes opened and she smiled up at him. Passion still in her stare, he held her gaze.

"I love you, more," he whispered to her.

With that, he turned on to his back and held her close to him. Satisfied and exhausted they fell asleep.

*****

The morning sun met his eyes closed with beautiful colors beneath his eyelids. The soft body next to his inched closer for his warmth. Alarmed, he slowly opened his eyes and his heart plummeted to his stomach. It was broad daylight and he was still in Emilia's room. He slowly lifted his head and looked around only to catch two pairs of doey eyed servants looking at him.

Sarah and Gertrude !!!.

Who knows how long they have been standing there.

He looked down at Emilia, sound asleep, he smiled. It was the first time he has woken up beside her. The lovestruck sighs from the maids made him roll his eyes. Slowly he raised his hands to his lips for them to not make a sound. Gently he sat up, looking at their eyes now widening at his nude state, he pulled the sheets up to his chest with a scowl. Twirling his fingers for them to turn around, he waited for them to do so and he quickly pulled on his breeches.

After a while of small whispers, they said the Duke was still in the house. Now with Emilia awake and nervous the morning became a show, an utter debacle. A tap came at her door with her aunt bidding entry. What unfolded before Emilia sent her into a wave of panic that she began to giggle uncontrollably at how they scampered about figuring out what to do with Dominic.

Quickly Gertrude gestured for him to squeeze under the bed. With shoving him and throwing his belongings with him. They quickly surrounded Emilia on the bed that at the moment could not stop laughing. Now coughing and red in the face her aunt upon entering the room, took her state as being ill.

Looking at her, she neared the bed and felt her forehead with the back of her hand.

"Mon Coeur, you do not have a fever. But, you are severely flushed." Her French accent was so beautiful and endearing.

Sadly, she brushed Emilia's hair from her face and held her chin up to get a better look at her.

"I guess you will not be able to go with us to Madam Claire's Brunch?" she asked.

With a soft nod and another cough, Emilia could not bare the closeness, embarrassed her cheeks reddened more.

"Very well, you stay in bed do not over work yourself." she looked sternly at the maids.

I will over work her alright. Dominic smirked, laying beneath the bed shaking his head.

"She stays in bed, eh!" She gave them a warning stare.

"We will see you later, today we will be out most of the day till the night." She turned to look at Emilia.

With quick nods, they agreed.

With a soft kiss on each cheek, she gave Emilia one last concerned glance before leaving.

Following her to the door Sarah waited for a while, then locked it.

Relief and fright washing over her, she leaned against the door and let out her breath, watching Gertrude and Emilia breathe and plop down on the bed.

Dominic finally crawled out from under the bed only to give Emilia a gaze that had her in a fit of laughter again. Shaking his head, he scrambled to her on the bed and began tickling her. Gertrude and Sarah sat back and giggled at the two. It was a breath of fresh air to see two souls such as them in such a state.

With that knowledge they waited for her aunt and uncle to leave. He stayed long enough to eat breakfast with her. Which was the best start of his morning ever. With one last kiss for the day until he saw her again, he left.

*****

The word was out and although it was sad, indeed the Duke was ill and was taking the turn for the worst. Lady Hannah was a young vibrant woman still in her prime not yet ready to settle with the fate she was cruelly delt. Her eyes were set on Dominic McAllister and she was going to have him. The lustful trysts' and the fierce desire he had felt for her were not going to die down so soon for some stupid little chit like Emilia Westham. She has come too far to let him slip through her fingers. She had to put some movement in motion to get her out of the way. She stood naked before the mirror eyeing the woman before her.

Long muscular fingers found their way around her waist and glided down between her thighs. Leaning her head against the shoulders that cradled her, she watched her image being stroked. Her breasts squeezed and her nipples teased and rubbed.

The fingers between her thighs rubbed her bud in a circular motion; she let out a soft moan.

Grey eye's looked at her image enjoying his handy work, watching her melt before him. He walked her over to a nearby table and pulled her leg up and leaned her forward taking her from behind. His thrusts were hard and rough just like she liked it, She begged him for it. He yanked and pulled her hair as he drove her into a climax with his roughness. With a whimper, her wetness tightened around his cock.

"Oh! Adam" she cried out in a pant.

With a groan heavy with lust, he slammed into her letting out a curse spilling his seed into her.

Still breathless, he pulled away from her and stretched out on his bed. She turned trembling leaning against the table and looked at him.

A little hurt that he showed her no type of affection or the least a caress.

Slowly she went to pick up her dress before he yanked her and pulled her onto the bed with him.

She looked an absolute mess and he mockingly pointed that out to her.

Scowling she yanked her arms away and stood from the bed getting dressed.

Silently he looked at her.

"So what was it you wanted to talk to me about?" he broke their silence.

Standing bolt upright, she contemplated her words.

"The night of your aunts ball, I saw you dancing with a girl," she breathed heavily.

Smirking at her, he gave a smile.

"I danced with many girls that night. Why do you mention it?" he paused. Then gave a devilish grin.

"Are we jealous, m'lady? "

Shaking her head, she turned to face him.

"You danced with Emilia Westham. Do you remember her?" She asked a bit agitated.

"Ah yes! She is beauty. I would not mind getting my hands on her" He smiled.

He watched Hannah's nose flare in anger.

He looked at her sideways.

"Why do you ask?"

She turned around to look away.

"I want you to court her; I want her out of the way far from Dominic."

He let out a hearty laugh at her ridiculous request.

"You're ordering me to court her?" he laughed with an incredulous stare.

Turning, she angrily answered.

"Yes," she hissed.

"Your husband's corpse has barely cooled in the ground and yet you are making plans to be with your lover?" he laughed.

She stood silently.

"Besides, I don't see why you would bother with him. It clearly shows he has interests elsewhere. I would not even doubt if it's one of the Jennings twins. That Margo is fire, there is just something about a red head in bed that gets you..." he shivered then smiled.

"Pure speculation and gossip." she fumed.

He yanked and pulled her struggling into his lap.

"Besides, what makes you think he would want you? It's been three months since he last touched you, am I correct,"

She did not answer.

"And, what is in it for me, what do I gain?"

She frantically searched her mind for that answer.

Hesitating ,she looked at him.

"Your gambling debt... I will pay it all off for you." She sat nervously in his lap watching his eyes turn to an icy steel.

With a harsh grip, he grabbed her hair and pulled her close.

"I do this you are going to pay my debt and much more. As you may know I am one for a VERY lavish lifestyle."

She silently waited for him to continue tears running down her cheeks.

"And, if this does not go as planned m'lady, I'm going to let Dominic know what a whore you really are, that he was not the only one slamming you. We were just the few of the men you fucked."

Angrily, she lashed out at him. He tossed her on the bed on her back and lay above her lifting her skirts he forcefully separated her legs.

Wetting his cock with her wetness, he placed it between her thighs. Pressing hard she tried to push on his chest, but he pinned her down and push it in. With a cry, she ground her face into his shoulder and whimpered. He thrust hard reveling in her moaning.

Yanking her head back by her hair, pulling her close, he whispered in her ears.

"I wonder what he would say once I confess to him about how you have been slobbering all over my cock, and that your pussy has been used so much its tightness has gone."

He slammed hard into her all the way to the hilt of his shaft that she squealed.

Finally, he reached his climax.

Quickly he stood from the bed and got dressed.

He turned to look at her, she lay curled up crying.

Ignoring her, he finished getting dressed.

"Fix yourself you look a mess, and hurry you must leave before anyone notices you."

Chapter 17

By next few days, it seemed like the huntress was on the prowl now that her mate was indisposed. Lady Hannah was not a sitting duck on the matter and she was determined to get what she wanted.

It was a little after midmorning when she pulled up near Dominic's home. The prying eyes were lacking today.

Dressed in her most beautiful gown she gave her bosoms one last push upward in her bodice to enticing swells. With that, she stepped out with the assistance of her footman. Climbing the stairs, she knocked on the door. The emotionless face of Bufford came into view and changed immediately to annoyance and disdain.

She barged in with a huff and walked past him with an upturned nose. Walking into the foyer, he skidded to a halt. Dressed and ready to leave, he was a bit miffed that Bufford let her in. But, dismissed the notion knowing how Hannah was.

"Darling!" she pulled him into a kiss and pawed him all up in a heated desire.

Bothered and in a rush to get her out of the house, he sighed.

"M'lady, I'm off to run some errands" he lied. He pulled her hands from around his neck.

"Well, maybe I can come with," She held on to his arms.

Stepping back a bit Dominic looked into her eyes, decided to tell her he was not interested in her anymore. It was evident now; he looked at her and could not see a reason to continue with her.

Before he could speak, Bufford interrupted him announcing another visitor.

Dominic looked up from Hannah's eyes at the front door. A bit bothered for being interrupted he gave Bufford a cold irritating stare, he could have sworn the old man smirked with satisfaction.

His heart stopped at the image before him. Hannah noticed him stiffen near her and watched his eyes widen to the person behind her. Quickly Hannah turned to face what would be the destruction of her.

Emilia!

The enchantress came into view and she was magnificent.

He could not believe what he was seeing.

She wore the most daring dress that caressed her curves. Her bodice sinfully low, barely contained her pert breasts.

A lump formed in his throat as he looked into her eyes and something in her stare made his cock jump. His eyes swept down to her pointy sensual high-heeled boots that gave her height to the added attraction. Her eyes held his like if they were the only two in the room. Green eyes trailed his body as she slowly walked towards him.

And when she spoke.

His hearing was surely deceiving him.

"My love, I see we haven't thrown out the trash yet," she pressed her body to his and glided one finger down his lips to his chin.

Hannah's gasp did not deter her.

She turned a teasing glare to Hannah and smiled as if acknowledging her for the first time.

"Oh! Lady Hannah, I am so sorry to hear about the Duke. I pray that he makes a speedy recovery."

Looking at Dominic again, his eyes were gleaming with surprise and lust. Her eyes were twinkling with mischief.

She lowered her gaze and walked towards the steps and he under her trance followed her.

She turned and placed her hand on his chest and leaned close to his ear and whispered.

"It would be wise if you sent her on her way," her lips neared his ears taking his earlobe into her lips and she flicked her hot tongue in it.

He groaned closing his eyes.

Opening them slowly he watched her walk up the steps. Hungry eyes watched those delicious hips sway out of his sight. He let out a guttural moan.

Letting out a shaky breath, he turned to face Hannah's heated glare.

She was livid.

He tried to figure out the words to tell her to leave, but no intelligible word could come out of his mouth, his heart would not stop thumping in his ears. To his salvation Bufford came into view and did it for him.

With a few insults, she walked off.

He bowed his head and closed his eyes, trying hard to control himself.

This vixen was surely undoing his sanity and be the death of him...

*****

She stood for a while looking out the window. With a smile, she watched Lady Hannah stomp her way into the waiting carriage right after she slapped Bufford's extended hand to help her get in.

The click of the door behind her made her smile even bigger.

She slowly turned to look at Dominic.

He had the smile of a man enjoying an intriguing game.

Hungry eyes watched her.

She trailed her finger on a book on his desk.

Her eyes flirted shamelessly with his.

He walked closer to his desk and clasped his hands behind his back. He was gorgeous, with taut muscular legs that stood their ground. She gave thanks silently to Lady Hannah for tousling him up a bit, leaving him more delicious than ever. His shirt lay wide open with a beautiful view of muscled abs and a strong chest.

He enjoyed how her eyes took their fill of his body.

With a seductive smile, he looked at her.

"You have my undivided attention m'lady," his voice sexy and low.

She slowly closed the distance between them.

"M'lord?" Coy green gems looked up at him seductively from hooded long lashes sensually licking her lips.

"I found a book in my uncle's study." her eyes hungrily looked at his lips.

He inched closer.

"Hmm, you did?" He moaned close to her lips.

"It was a book about the art of love making," her eyes glided up to his.

Peeked with intrigue his eyes held her gaze while she continued.

"It had a lot of...pictures," her fingers trailed his throat.

She grinned at the sign of his racing pulse beneath her touch.

"There was one picture in particular that I liked," She glided her hand down until it reached the button to his breeches.

He watched her gently undo them.

A smile tugged at his lips.

"Really and what picture is that, m'lady," His voice like silk caressed her ear.

She went on to undo them slowly one by one.

He moaned when she leaned in to kiss his chest.

Astonished and in awe he watched her trail hot kisses down his his chest to his taut stomach.

She freed his cock from his breeches. Before he could put together her intention, Seductive emerald gems held his gaze and her tongue tasted him.

A curse slipped his lips.

He moaned, closing his eyes and his head fell back.

The feel of her warm lips there, was making his knees buckle.

She took him completely in her mouth and went on a rhythmic endeavor.

"Emilia? What are you doing to me?" he groaned aloud.

His heart pummeled in his chest, he was surely going to explode. Legs weakly held him up while she worked her magic on him.

He was at his breaking point, his body trembled with pressure building up ready for his release.

In a heart stopping moment midway through the torrent of pleasure, she stood up. Agony played on his senses because she toyed with him. His breath heavy, he leaned his forehead to hers. His blood roared in his ears.

His eyes opened to look into hers. Dark and dangerously gorgeous.

He bent to kiss her lips, but she turned her face, giving him her cheek. Confused, he frowned. Struggling with what just happened. Passion filled eyes met seductive sexy gems of mischief and triumph. Her lips close to his ears whispered.

"I want to savor the taste of you on my lips, m'lord" the delicious tip of her tongue glided over her lips.

In that instant, she slipped sweetly from between him and the table and softly walked towards the door.

Dominic still holding his breeches, still breathless and trembling turned to lean for support on the table. He watched the temptress that she is, turn and give him the most sexiest wink ever, and skillfully leave him standing there hot and ready for sex.

Touche'

Payback that was well overdue!!!

The minx worked him good.

He let out a breathless laugh mesmerized and in disbelief.

*****

They continued their secret romantic encounters. However, neither of them was prepared for what was to come. It will be turmoil in the making that will surely change all of their lives.

Something was brewing and she could feel it. The morning was not its usual one. Gertrude entered with a not to convincing smile and woke her up. Puzzled Emilia sat up and studied Gertrude's expression.

"Gertrude what is wrong?" Emilia sat up in bed worried.

Sad Gertrude turned to her and looked at her, hesitating to tell her.

"Oh! tis not my place to say child," Gertrude twirled her skirts in her finger.

"Come, you must get dressed your uncle is waiting for you in the study" she whispered.

Nervously Emilia began to shake, her pulse racing.

"Oh no!!Does he know? Does he know about Dominic and.."

Before she could finish Sarah rushed in.

"You are not dressed?"

Before she could get another word out they began laying out her beautiful gowns. They picked the most elegant one.

"I want you to listen to me Emilia." Sarah turned her around fast.

"Your uncle is in his study with Adam VanCamp, Lord Evers. We are not sure of his visit, but you must keep a calm air about you." She warned.

Sarah swirled her back around and looked her in her eyes.

"Can you do that?" Sarah asked.

Nodding slowly she turned back around and looked herself in the mirror. She felt nothing like the person in the mirror. Silently she walked out of her room down the steps into the hall. She tapped lightly until hearing her uncle's voice to enter.

Entering the large study, she walked until she was beside his desk. He motioned for her to sit.

She was introduced to Adam VanCamp to her right.

He offered a debonair smile that she returned as well.

"Emilia, Lord VanCamp here has come to ask my permission to court you. I feel he is a very good match so I have decided to do up an early marriage contract. We will set the date for three months."

Silently she sat staring at nothing.

Her ears were deceiving her, she could not have heard correctly.

Three months?.

Her uncle watched her and grew a concerned look.

"Emilia!"

She blinked up at him lost and confused with what was going on.

"Three month's?" She repeated.

She lowered her gaze to hide the tears in her eyes.

She smoothed her skirt before her and folded her hands trying to regain her composure.

She looked beside her to Adam. Her eyes immediately met his.

He was dressed to perfection. Very handsome.

He gave her a beautiful smile.

Silently they stared at each other.

*****

He watched her carefully. She was very beautiful. She sat quietly with her head bent and fingers crossed. Petite and demure as he could see. She had long chestnut brown hair in beautiful ringlets down her back. Gorgeous green eyes with long lashes, pert nose with pretty lips.

Their silent observation of one another was interrupted.

"I believe I will leave you two to get acquainted, I will be in the dining room."

He walked around the table to leave the study. The soft click of the door was the last thing heard before the room fell silent again.

"You're very lovely today, Emilia" his voice was low.

She looked at him.

"Thank you" She replied.

Not knowing what else to say she slowly stood. Trying to muster up the courage to talk to him even though she really did not want to.

"M'lord? ..." she whispered.

"Please, no mean for titles call me, Adam," he said softly standing behind her.

She turned to look at him.

"What made you decide to choose me?" She asked with a sad tone.

For a moment, he was thrown back with her question then looked at her puzzled.

"Because from the moment I saw you, I was smitten by you. You're very beautiful." He grinned.

Silently she stood with a very gloomy look on her face.

He came very close to her and she nervously inched back.

Tipping her chin up gently, he looked into her eyes. They were sad and red with unshed tears.

"I know this is too soon, but, you must understand it is what your uncle wants. And, I am honored that he chose me." He caressed her cheek.

"But, what about what I want? She stepped away.

"The decision was made without my knowledge. You don't even know me, yet I am to marry you in three months" She cried.

She turned and ran off.

"Emilia, wait," he called after her.

"This could not be happening," she thought.

She closed the door to her room. She shut the world out with her cries. She was to marry someone she did not love. She would never be with Dominic again. The thought of losing him was too painful. She lay on her bed and cried into her pillow until she had no more tears to spill. She closed her eyes wanting to sleep, to drown out all that was happening.

The day went on and she ate nothing for lunch. Supper time came around and she did not move. Her head spun with the stress of it all. She wanted to give up. If she could not be with Dominic, then why exist?

******

The news came to him like a punch to the stomach. She was to marry another. He sat and heard the gossip at the men's club where Adam, Lord Evers sat and boasted about his union with Emilia Westham and the wedding was to take place in three months. How was this possible? The hurrahs, hoops and congratulations wrung freely amongst the men. Dimitri sat before him, eyeing him and giving him a warning glare to not do anything crazy.

They watched as the young man was hugged and heavy slaps on the back were exchanged.

"You nailed a good catch you sly devil." a man said.

With a chuckle, Adam nodded his head.

The conversation went on about how since his first dance with her he knew he had to have her.

If he only knew he had her first Dominic thought smugly.

He wanted to stand and declare that he loved her. That they loved each other. His head was beginning to ache with this sudden news.

He stood quickly and was stopped by Dimitri.

"I must go to her, she must be suffering."

Dimitri looked into his friend's eyes. The look in them told him he was determined to see her tonight. With a nod Dimitri moved out of his way and Dominic left.

*****

The night could not have come any quicker. He watched two sets of sad eyes meet him at the door. They whispered on their way up the stairs.

"She has not eaten all day m'lord " Gertrude sniffled.

With a nod, he rubbed her shoulder and looked at Sarah dashing away a tear from her eye.

He opened the door, closed it behind him and locked it. He immediately removed his long coat, vest and boots. He padded softly to the bed. She slept with her back to him. Softly he slipped beneath the sheets and pulled her close to him. He buried his face in the lushness of her hair and its sweet smell. She stirred in her sleep a bit then woke up to the feel of him. She turned to face him and his warm embrace just when she thought she had cried all she could earlier, the torrent of tears fell again.

Throughout the night, he caressed her and reassured her that all was going to be ok. A lie he had to believe in because at that point he realized this might be their last night together and he did not think he could handle that truth. As harsh, as it was he could not handle it. But, he had to choose her happiness or his selfish need to have her regardless of the outcome. It was a risk he had to take, it was for the best that with a heavy heart he had to put some distance between them.

If you love someone, set them free. If they come back they're yours; if they don't they never were.

With that decision burned into his mind, he made love to her for the very last time.

Chapter 18

W eeks had passed, and their courting went as planned. Adam, was the epitome of a gentlemen. He was sweet and polite. But, regardless of it all , Emilia with all her might her heart belonged to Dominic. She had not seen him in some time and she was severely worried.

The news of the Dukes death was a stagnant gossip that would not go away and the notion of her wedding to Adam would give The Duchess free reign to be with Dominic. And the idea sickened her.

So lost in her thoughts she never heard Adam come near her. His touch broke her free of her gripping thoughts only to meet his stern gaze.

"What are we daydreaming about, my beauty?" he looked down at her.

She blinked twice taking in the view of him. With the sweetest smile she could give him, she shook her head.

"Nothing," She looked into his skeptical glare before averting her eyes.

With a sigh, he sat beside her.

Silently he sat with her.

"I feel you distant and it is unnerving, Emilia" he said agitated.

She said nothing.

"If we are to be married we need to have some semblance of a loving relationship."

He looked at her.

She could feel the heat of his gaze on her.

Nodding, she slowly stood.

Before she could walk away, his strong hand in a tightening squeeze pulled her in to his lap.

Astonished by his iron grip, her struggle to get free stopped at his heated glare. There was something in his eyes that sent a warning shiver up her spine.

"I will be leaving for Wales within the hour and I will return in 2 weeks." His stare grew serious.

"When I return you will be the most devoted and loving fiancée ever. You will come to terms with this marriage and accept it with delight and enthusiasm."

He tightened his grip around her arm. His other hand tightened around her waist.

She could not believe what she was hearing. Frightened, tears began to fall.

"So you have two weeks to get all of the woes of your lost lover out of your heart, because in my marriage to you Emilia, I will not be taken for a fool." He warned.

She shot him a surprised look.

The grin that formed on his lips and the stare in his eyes made her fidget a little in his grip. She averted her gaze.

He lifted his hand to caress her neck and was satisfied with the feel of her racy pulse. He caressed her cheek and turned it to face her. Their eyes met and the nearness of their breaths collided. His lips crushed hers with a possessive kiss, with her hands she pushed against his chest. But, his grip was stronger. Pulling her head back, he looked her in the eyes. Amused at the little fight in her and fire in her eyes, it peaked his interest of just how much fight he could get out of her.

"Remember, Two weeks to do as you please pretty much. If you have to fuck your lover enough to assuage your need I will turn a blind eye." he grinned provocatively.

Her face turned red with embarrassment.

She looked away. Her heart raced with worry that he knew she was not a virgin anymore. Before she could finish thinking and collectively taking in his words, he spoke again. And whispered in her ear.

"Two weeks, remember and when I return this ...your coldness towards me will end."

With that he let her stand from his knees. He stood and gripped her chin tightly and brought her lips to his in a rough kiss that left her lips bruised and swollen.

With a wink, he turned and walked off.

Now alone her body wracked with a mixture of fright and anger. She could not stop shaking, she sat in tears back on the bench. Her life as she knew it, was doomed. She cried into her shaking hands.

******

It was a decision Dominic toyed with for days and his heart ached more and more with what he must do.

Dominic looked at Dimitri's reproaching gaze.

"Why, would you do such a thing" he shook his head.

Lulled by the effects of the whiskey he dragged his hands thru his hair and leaned his head on the desk.

Now bedraggled, infuriated and drunk blue pools of misery stared at Dimitri.

"She needs to be happy," he shrugged his shoulder, not able to think of any other explanation.

"Aye, with another man?" Dimitri asked sarcastically.

"Has it not occured to you brother, that the woman you love in a matter of mere weeks, will no longer be yours."

Dimitri waited for Dominic to react.

The slight tap at the door broke his next question when Bufford entered announcing Emilia was here.

He sadly looked at her and let her walk in.

Dominic composed himself and sat up. Hiding the love he felt for her beneath a cold emotionless stare.

"Come in Ms. Westham" he spoke.

Immediately Dimitri gave her a sweet warm smile before excusing himself to leave them alone.

Silently she sat and looked in her lap.

"I haven't seen you in a while." Her soft voice broke the silence.

His heart sank when he finally focused on her.

Her face was pale and her eyes bleak.

Immediately his look changed when she looked at him.

"I have been busy." he said dryly.

With a nod she looked again at him but his cold demeanor saddened her.

He turned his gaze and focused on the book before him. His heart raced with what he was going to say, but he had to, it was for the best.

"Emilia........it's best if we were distanced," he breathed.

Her eyes looked at him confused.

"But..."

"You will be getting married soon and we can never see each other again," he breathed.

Flustered and sad her eyes filled with tears, she looked down.

"Just like that you expect me to accept that." her eyes filled with tears.

"You must." he looked away.

"Well I won't. I love you." her tears fell.

"Well I don't " his lie so fast poured out he prayed the painful sting of it would convince her otherwise.

Like a slap to the face, she stood looking into his eyes lost for words.

"I don't love you, I thought I did but I made a mistake." he paused trying to regain a grip on his composure.

"What happened between us was a mistake, Emilia." he stood giving her his back. He couldn't look her in the eyes.

She began to cry and it pulled at his heart. She stood up from the chair. Her heart heavy with pain began to slam into her chest violently.

"Why are you doing this to me?" her was voice shaky and breathless.

He turned to look at her.

"Forgive me I wasn't thinking," he watched her.

Her eyes filled with hurt looked away. Right away her breathing increased with her cry. She felt so sick and weak that her legs could barely hold her up. His heart sank when he saw her sway. Alarmed he panicked.

"Emilia!"

She fell to her knees her vision blurry and head spinning she felt Dominic holding her.

She lashed out immediately and pulled away, but he wouldnt let her.

She slapped him.

The sting of her hands and thwack across the face left him stunned.

She stood on shaky legs.

"I hate you, Don't you ever touch me again." She struggled against him.

"I damn the day I ever met you," she pulled away.

He stared into her eyes and what once before held love for him, now looked at him with hurt and anger.

Her hand touched her forehead and her eyes fluttered shut.

He quickly caught her before she collapsed to the floor. He cradled her in his arms and he could not contain his emotions any longer.

He cried.

He smoothed her hair back from her face and took in her features. She was thin and pale, Her fingers icy cold. The result of her unhappiness was evident. And he made it worse. With a curse he stood with her feather light weight in his arms and walked with her out of his study. The astonished eyes of Bufford and Dimitri grew concerned.

"Good Lord, man! What did you do?" Dimitri asked following him up the stairs.

"She fainted," he hissed.

"From what you said? because we heard all of it and you were cruel, Dominic"

Dimitri argued with him until he reached his room and he continued their argument after placing her on his bed.

"Damn it! Dimitri, understand this is hard for me as well." he yelled.

" Look at her, and look you Dominic. Does it look like she is taking this well?" Dimitri shook his head.

"You just told the love of your life; you never loved her and that what you both had was a mistake," he stared incredulously at Dominic

Dominic closed his eyes in shame at his own words being repeated to him. He turned his back on Dimitri. Bufford entered with some smelling salts and water quickly to attend to Emilia.

Dimitri with a curse quickly stomped off and left.

Not understanding Dominic's decision to push Emilia away. They were both suffering. He had to find a way to help them out before things got worse.

Dominic stood and watched as Bufford waved the small vile under Emilia's nose. With a cough, she stirred awake. Confused she looked around and closed her eyes. Bufford whispered soft words to her and offered her water. She trembled while taking the glass and drank very little of it. She begged Bufford to help her up and take her to her carriage. She never looked his way, never acknowledged his concerned stare. She walked out and never looked back. Anger and pain coursed through Dominic's veins that he grabbed the first thing before him and with a roar of rage, he threw it. Shattered glass was everywhere from the glass left on the table. Falling to his knees, he slammed his fists into the floor. He buried his hands in his face and wept.

He lost her for good.

Chapter 19

The gossip spread like wildfire that The Duchess and Marquee were an item. She didn't even wait for her husband's corpse to cool in his grave before she laid a claim to the Marquess of Grisham. She felt sick at the news, her heart raced furiously in her chest and she felt a little faint.

Gertrude stood by her side at the supper table noticing how she ate very little and in the mornings how she wretched mercilessly.

When supper was over she walked up to her room exhausted of her false facade. Sarah joined her after and helped her undress. She gasped at the sight of Emilia's body.

Although frail from lack of food and sleep, Emilia's breasts seemed larger and her waist thicker.

Weary tired eyes looked at Sarah's

"What is it?" she hugged her self, ashamed of Sarah's eyes looking over her.

"Em? When is the last time you have seen your menses." Sarah looked up to Emilia's tired eyes, worried.

Lost for words she blushed. Truth is she could not remember because it rarely came. She sadly shook her head confused.

"I do not know, why do you ask?" her voice barely audible with weakness.

She rest her hands on Emilia's waist.

"Emilia you're with child!!!" she whispered softly her eye's slowly rose to look at her.

Hugging herself she stepped back shaking her head she scowled.

"I can't be, I am not." she furiously looked away.

She turned and closed her eyes. Gently she placed her hand on her abdomen. How can this be?

Tears fell as she stood staring into nothing...

"We must tell Lord Dominic," Sarah whispered.

Emilia slowly turned and frantically shook her head.

"He can not know, Sarah," Emilia cried softly.

"Promise me you won't, It will ruin us both," She held Sarah' gaze.

Heartache and Sadness stared at Sarah. She tried earnestly to convince Emilia to tell him. But, she refused.

Not wanting to talk anymore, Emilia went to bed anxious to drown out the world with her tears and sleep.

******

Sarah, Gertrude and Bufford sat quietly in a sad silence.

"Are you sure?" Bufford looked sternly at Gertrude and Sarah.

The two showed up late at his doorstep quietly he snuck them in through the back and they sat in the kitchen whispering over tea.

"Of course I'm sure! She has missed her menses, her hips have widened and she has had morning sickness for the past few days." Gertrude worriedly explained.

They exchanged frantic gazes waiting for him to speak.

"We must tell the Marquess," He decided.

"We cannot, t'is not our place. Besides, he clearly pushed her away," Gertrude shook her head disappointed .

"And what do you pretend we do, sit back and wait for her to show, or let another man claim m'lord's heir as his own?" he tried to quiet the rage in his voice.

"He loves her too much to let her marry another man carrying his child," Bufford pointed out the obvious.

"She is to marry Lord VanCamp in two more months, what are we to do?" Sarah cried nervously.

Unawares to them, prying ears heard it all.

She heard the whispers coming down for water.That little bitch is pregnant !!! she fumed.

She never suspected Dominic had gone that far with the whelp. He has been distant with her, his lovemaking was not the same. She needed to rush things along for her and Dominic so Adam could marry her and take her away.

She turned and padded slowly up the stairs quietly.

******

Her stroll through the park with Gertrude was somewhat relaxing. She enjoyed the brisk cool air and wind that flowed thru her hair.

Her 17th birthday had come and passed. It was celebrated with little enthusiasm. For as much as her uncle and aunt tried, she kindly turned down any festivities they planned for her.

On a good note her heartache slowly began to wither away. She came to terms with her fate and accepted it head on. She was pregnant and terrified for the most part.

Gertrude's hands tightened around Emilia's arm pulling her thoughts away with the pain.

She looked at Gertrude and followed her eyes to the person walking before them. Before she could coolly ignore her, the menacing glare of Lady Hannah came into view.

"Why, Emilia! What a charm seeing you this early in the park." She put on her fakest smile.

Emilia displayed her broadest smile yet.

"Thank you milady, same to you," Emilia held her gaze with Hannah's for a while.

Clearing her throat, Hannah looked at them both.

"May I speak alone with Emilia?"

She gave a warning glare to Gertrude.

Before Emilia could answer, Gertrude lowered her head and stepped back.

Emilia frowned and stepped back as Hannah came close and wrapped her arms around Emilia's pulling her into a slow walk.

The harsh squeeze was a warning to follow.

Gertrude trailed nervously behind them.

Silently she walked aware of her surroundings.

"Tell me Emilia, how are we fairing as of late," Hannah spoke with her eyes looking forward.

"My well being is not your affair," Emilia bit out.

"When it threatens my future it is very much my affair," she hissed.

"What are you getting at?" irritated Emilia pulled her arm from Hannah's grip.

"Come now you little bitch! your pregnant with Dominic's child, and I will not let your bastard child come in the way of my happiness," Hannah spoke thru clenched teeth.

"Don't let my child be an excuse for your happiness, Hanna. You have what you want, so leave me the hell alone," Emilia strained against shedding tears and anger.

Before she turned to walk off Hannah stopped her in her tracks.

"For a coy bitch you really know how to hide things, I would never have thought the tons wallflower would be so cunning as to have a speedy marriage in time to pass off another man's child on her betrothed. Now that is rich," She let out a hearty laugh.

"I suggest a good fitting bodice should help. Remember to keep one handy," She mocked looking at Emilia's abdomen.

The ire in Emilia's stare was evident as she walked closer ,stood before Hannah and slapped her so hard that Gertrude flinched and covered her chest in fear.

"You listen to me m'lady, when you're lying beneath Dominic and he is making sweet love to you, remember it is me who he is thinking of. It is me who he loves, not you. Do not temp me to drop this bit of news before him of me carrying his child, because you will surely loose this battle," she bit out enraged.

Walking off she left a dishelved Hannah staring at her astonished, rubbing her stinging red cheek.

Chapter 20

Lord Darcy of Glover was hosting a party and invited all to attend. A simple gathering for drinks, cocktails, and dancing. All the who's who would be there no doubt she sighed. She thought she could escape this one, but as her uncle pointed out it will be two more days before Adam returned after that she would not be attending balls and parties alone.

With the help of Sarah and Gertrude, she dawned the most fetching elegant Royal blue gown that looked so beautiful on her.

Arriving she was helped out of the carriage accompanying her uncle as usual she walked beside him.

The gasps, awes and broad smiles made her blush.

Although she did not see him, he saw her and his eyes softened.

She was exquisite, gorgeous and breathtaking.

He hadn't seen her in almost two weeks and it felt like an eternity. She was alone and he wanted a moment with her.

The soft squeeze of his arm brought his eyes to look into Hannah's stare it was obvious she knew where his attention was. Trying effortlessly to smile and be loving to her, he couldn't. It was the worst day of his life.

Hannah revealed to him she was pregnant. Shocked and disappointed he put on his best smile and kissed her. But he felt no joy in his heart. He would eventually have to marry her to avoid bringing a bastard child into this world. He was miserable and mad at himself for letting this situation get out of control.

Many began to dance and soon everyone was enthralled with the evening's merriment. He put on his game face and pretended to be enjoying his company with Hannah and another couple. He took advantage of her conversation with them to make an excuse to bring them all back more punch.

His eyes needed to adjust to the outside darkness. He searched the ample garden and spotted her. She hugged her self lost in her own thoughts she never heard him come close.

"It is a beautiful night is it not." the huskiness of his voice broke the silence.

She stiffened.

She turned to look at him.

Although she could see little of him in the moonlight, she could tell he was very handsome tonight. He came closer and she stepped back. His nearness only increased her desire for him.

"Why are you here," her voice shaky.

"I had to see you, talk to you, ...hold you," he breathed.

"You said what was between us was a mistake, Dominic," her voice cracked.

He shook his head. "I lied... I want you, I love you," He inched closer.

She stepped away from him.

"You made it abundantly clear that we needed to put distance between us and I did what you asked. Now I ask that you do the same." she cried out.

Trying to walk off, he caught her and pulled her close.

"I need you." his breath mingled with hers.

She pushed him away.

"No... You do not get to toss me aside and when you want, you pick me back up Dominic!" She shoved his chest in tears.

"It was a mistake remember? you never loved me, were your words," She yelled accusingly, breaking free of his hold.

"Yes, as were your words Emilia, you damned the day we ever met." he argued back.

She turned to walk off again.

He trailed after her.

"You seem to deal the blows, but you cannot take them," She whirled and screamed at him.

"What do you want from me?" Her tears fell like waterfalls.

"I want you, damn it" He cried out.

"Well you cannot, I am not yours to have, I belong to another." she cried out in sobs.

"The hell you do, you belong to me Emilia Westham, only me,"

He pulled her close to him in a strong embrace and claimed her lips in searing hot kiss of longing and desire.

Her struggles were useless against his hold as he squeezed and caressed her with so much need.

"We cannot do this Dominic, " she cried out before he claimed her lips again.

He thanked God they were far out in the massive garden far from the party, secluded from everyone and the prying ears.

He leaned her up a nearby tree. He trailed hot kisses up and down her neck over the top of her breasts. He reached beneath her skirts and rubbed hotness between her thighs; she clung to him and whimpered so sweetly.

He quickly undid his breeches and removed her undergarment. Unable to stop him she gave into his pleasure, his touch and the need of him.

He wrapped her legs around his waist his hardness plunged into her and he moaned her name between sobs. They kissed and she felt his tears mingle with hers on their lips. His rhythm with each thrust had heat crawling over her. Her pants and whimpers were sweetness to his ears.

They whispered their love for one another between ardent kisses and sobs. Weak with desire she reached the peak of her climax her insides clenched and he thrust harder, deeper he moaned out her name shuddering with his release.

She clung to him breathless, weak and satisfied. Their breaths mingled.

"Know this Emilia, as long as my heart still beats in my chest, I will never let you go," still holding her tightly he looked at her and held her gaze.

She closed them and lowered her head in defeat not able to respond. He would never let her go. He softly let her down.

Deep down he wanted to take her again and make love to her.

Silently they dressed and fixed themselves up.

She stood with her back to him.

Still shaking and overwhelmed from their fight and lovemaking.

She couldn't marry Adam but she had no choice, she couldn't be with Dominic either.

She began to cry.

He pulled her into his arms and kissed her forehead.

She pulled away and ran towards the entrance of the garden, but his warm arms caught her.

Her struggles only tightened his grip more.

"Don't run from me," he hoarsely demanded.

"You must let me go. I must live my life and you must live yours," she pleaded struggling to free herself from him.

"I would listen to her my love," Hannah came forward.

She stiffened hearing Hannah's voice.

She pulled away from Dominic.

Like a menacing snake Hannah neared his side and draped her hands around his arm pulling him close.

His jaw clenched.

"My love, you do realize she is getting married, right?" Hannah teased.

Emilia stepped back wanting to leave but Hannah stopped her long enough to deliver another blow.

"My love, did you not tell her we are expecting our first child?"

Confused Emilia stood looking at them both backing away lowering her head she walked off.

"Emilia wait" he called after her.

Hannah furiously pulled him from following Emilia.

"I will not be made a fool of Dominic, you are with me."

"Then know your place, you are not my wife," he hissed dangerously backing her up with a murderous glare.

"But I am carrying your child," she angrily whispered.

"And she carries my heart," he yelled furiously.

He yanked away his arm and went to follow Emilia.

He caught a glimpse of her entering the ballroom swerving thru the guests trying to get away. As the music died down and changed some dancers cleared away while others walked out to start dancing. She walked half way onto the dance floor trying to cross to the other side to get away from Dominic. But she stopped midway. Dominic stopped behind her. He sensed something was wrong because he noticed another girl stood in stark fright staring at her.

"Joanna" she shook her head in disbelief.

He watched as the girl frantically looked for a way to escape.

Emilia closed the distance and slapped her hard wringing a cry from her. The music died down while onlookers gasped and they were all in awe at what unfolded before them.

Quickly Dominic held her arms to keep her from pummeling the girl before her.

In a heated rage he has never seen in Emilia she yelled.

"You are the reason for my misfortune you evil bitch," Her voice shook.

"You are the one that pushed me out of that carriage,"

The gasps everyone let out.

She watched The Earl run to Joanna's side and pulled her close giving Emilia a nasty glare.

Amused Emilia let out a laugh that was so unlike her.

"I see you still married the Earl any way and no doubt you made him believe the babe in your womb is his?." she looked at her swollen abdomen.

Joanna recoiled from Emilia's icy glare holding her stomach before she turned a guilty look at the Earl.

"Being married to you m'lord was not in my sister's plans. I found her with Stephen, my uncles stepson and to keep anyone from knowing about them she tried to kill me." Emilia cried.

"Emilia, what are you saying? Is this true, Johanna," her uncle came forward rift with anger.

Silently Johanna lowered her gaze as Ethan stood back looking at her in disgust.

"She had plans to run off with him, because she could not bare to be in the arms of that monster. Is that how you said it sister?" she let out a sob.

So much anger coursed thru Emilia that she began to tremble and Dominic could feel it.

"To satisfy your lust, because I am pretty sure you did none of it for love. You doomed my life Johanna, I am living in hell. You should have just tossed me in the water and left me for dead,"

She shouted with so much rage.

She yanked her arms away from Dominic breaking free from his hold and ran out of the ballroom.

Lowering his head, he hid his pain at Emilia's words.

A strong hand reached for his shoulder.

He turned to see Dimitri with the same sad look.

She rode away back home before anyone could stop her. Sarah greeted her with a smile that slowly disappeared in stark fright.

"Emilia what is wrong?." She followed her up the stairs to her room.

She stood and watched Emilia frantically pull clothing from her trunks and stuffed them in a bag.

"Em, what are you doing?"

"I am leaving, I cannot bare to be here anymore." she sobbed.

"Please, Emilia you're acting irrational you're not well." Sara pleaded.

Her mind was made up.

"Where are you going to go?" Sarah followed her about.

She stopped long enough to answer then bolted out the door.

"To stay with my grandfather"

Sarah stomped off behind her ready for an argument. "I am going with you."

"No, you are not"

"Either I go or I will go and tell Lord McAllister about everything," Sarah threatened.

She watched Emilia's eyes water again.

"You would betray me like that Sarah," Emilia frowned with hurt.

"If it means to keep you safe I will. So what will it be m'lady? Sarah stood her ground waiting for Emilia to decide.

Emilia sadly agreed and warned they needed to hurry.

They quickly walked out and climbed in the empty carriage left at the door with no driver in sight. Immediately Sarah took the reins and snapped the horses into a gallop. Emilia with tears watched all the buildings zip past her as they drove their way away from town.

Chapter 21

The night was a shamble, Emilia never showed up and all were growing worried with her disappearance. Morning had come and still no sign of her nor Sarah.

Weary eyes watched each other. Agony stricken eyes around the room nervously looked at the clock above the mantle.

The soft sobs of Gertrude together with the Duchess just made things more gloom. Dominic paced while her uncle sat with his face in his hands.

Irritated her uncle stood. "She has to be around here somewhere." He fumed.

"This is just like her to run off, I pray she returns before VanCamp does." He added.

Dominic's incredulous stare caught Dimitri but he was too late to stop Dominic.

"You heartless bastard is that all you are worried about?" Dominic yelled.

"I should have never brought her back here."

"How dare you speak to me that way" the Duke raged.

"All of this is your fault, you just had to force a marriage upon her for your own gain." Dominic croaked with pain in his voice.

Dimitri immediately pulled him back trying to calm his anger.

The duke immediately stood before him ready for a fight.

"What I do with my nieces' well being is of no concern to you, McAllister." The duke hissed.

Inching closer trembling with rage wracked with so much emotion and tears in his eyes.

"It concerns me because it pertains to the love of my life." His feral gaze turned dark.

At that moment, the duke paled and stepped back holding his chest in disbelief.

All stood in shock at his confession.

"You bastard, tell me you did not dishonor my niece?" Margave yelled.

Dominic stood his ground ready for the onslaught of his actions.

The duke lunged at him and the scuffle began. The Duchess nervously cried then fainted at what unfolded before her. Dimitri dodged flying fists and the blows trying to separate the men.

Finally, Dimitri pulled Dominic back and away from the heated glare of Margave

Fists still clenched and breathing heavily he faced Margave, "Know this old man; she is all that I hold dear to me, I love her. If anything happens to her it will only fall on your head"

Adamant on not leaving, he stayed waiting for some news of where Emilia was.

It was an agonizing wait and the still no sign of Emilia.

Dimitri stood and looked at Dominic.

"Do you think she could have returned to Grisham?"

Silently he thought, it could be possible.

"I will ready a carriage; will you stay in case she returns?" Dominic worried gaze eased as Dimitri agreed.

"Go with care brother, I will keep her safe if she returns"

Hours had passed when Dimitri sat with the Duke and they spoke. The tap on the door followed by Jeoffry stopped their conversation.

"Lord Evers has arrived, your grace."

With a brief nod, Jeoffry stepped aside for Adam to enter. The grim look on his face was evident that he knew what happened.

Dimitri stood and excused himself so they could talk.

"What happened?" Adam scowled.

Dimitri listened to the conversation and clearly saw from Van-Camps demeanor, the worry was vague. His only interest was that the Duke honored his end of the bargain. Turning his back away from the door, VanCamp stormed off without a backward glance.

With a suspicious feeling, he had to find out more about the man.

*****

Days had passed and while all worried one person in particular decided to be careless and eventually he got caught. For some time Dimitri's speculations about Adam were right. Although just a rumor, he had to see it for himself.

He owed a very high gambling dept that needed payment. But such a payment he would never get it from the Duke.

He was sure the Duke would never give in to it. His suspicions were still inconclusive so he continued to watch him. He stood outside of his home needing a way to get in. He would sneak in to find some evidence and be out quickly.

His search was fruitless.

The noise coming from below alarmed him. He hid in a near dark corner as the voices came closer. He watched in shock as VanCamp entered tumbling into his bedroom with a woman struggling. Shoving her into the room, he slammed the door shut.

Hannah? Dimitri was horrified and perplexed.

She stood frightened looking at him, in two strides he was before her and slapped her to the bed.

Dimitri wanted to bust out and punch him to the ground but didn't dare.

"Please, Adam I didn't know she would leave," Hannah cried out.

"You provoked her, why the hell would you tell McAllister you're with his child if it is not true. Do you think he won't figure it out you fool." Adam shouted.

"I was trying to get her out of his way, to get married with him" she sniffed.

"The deal was to help you by marrying her and in exchange you pay off my dept."

"I will" she pleaded.

"I still want her" Adam fumed.

"Well she is pregnant," Hannah lashed out.

Dimitri listened in shock, their plan to take the child and pass it off as her own, Hannah paying for his gambling dept in exchange to marry Emilia and the most shocking was she was sleeping with Adam. He watched how Adam ruthlessly like a dog ravished Hannah like if she were nothing, ordered her to dress and leave.

Before she walked off, he grabbed her by the neck and ordered her to pay the dept immediately. Enraged by all of this as soon as Hannah left, Dimitri revealed himself.

******

Tired old eyes watched the troubled girl sleep. His one and only grandchild was suffering. He should have never let her live with his son. The dolt had not an inch of knowledge or care in his heart for raising a child. He felt it would be better for her. She needed to be amongst peers of her own age. He realizes now it was a very bad idea.

Ferguson, Emilia's Grandfather was shocked and surprised to see her at his door and in such a condition, it enraged him that her own flesh and blood could cause this. She arrived with Sarah practically carrying her. In tears and heartbroken she hasn't slept or eaten well in the past several days. Sarah explained what she could but had no idea what happened so that she chose to return to Scotland.

"Your grace she is eating very little" Sarah stood next to Ferguson

"We must tell Lord McAllister, she needs him" she cried.

"Are ye sure he would come for her Sarah?" his eyes sadly turned to look at his granddaughter in the distance.

Sarah lowered her head dashing away a tear.

"They love each other deeply your grace and I fear he is suffering just as much as she at this moment, we disappeared in the night. No one knows where we are."

Emilia's grandfather watched from the entrance door to the bedroom. Emilia was sleeping by the large window overlooking the vast lush lands on the estate.

No one prepared her for this cruel game of love and heartache. He doesn't know how it came to this but it did and slowly it was slipping away with her life.

"I will go and find him, my granddaughter and great-grandchild will not die on me, he will not lose them," He shook his head.

*****

The days had passed and still no sign of Emilia or Sarah the worry was deep. Dominic could not sleep or think straight his heart worried, his nerves were on edge thinking of the worst.

Bufford tried his best to find out what he could but to no avail it was useless.

He paced back and forth, frantic thoughts roamed in his mind.

Where could she be?

Was she well?

All questions went unanswered and it unnerved him. He searched everywhere he could think of and he had nothing.

Dominic threw himself on a nearby chair furious.

Bufford entered looking at the hellish state of Dominic; it just made his heart sad. He drank himself to sleep, he went out all day in search but would return in such a foul mood.

"M'lord would you like anything?" Bufford looked at him.

The bothered look on Dominic's face unnerved him a bit.

"What I want Bufford is to find her, she is out there and we know nothing of her whereabouts," he croaked.

Bufford had the urge to tell him everything but he couldn't risk her being exposed, it would be detrimental.

Before he could speak, shouts and scuffles were heard in the foyer and coming nearer to his library. As Dominic stood exchanging a puzzled look at Bufford he neared the door but quickly stepped back as Dimitri busted thru holding another man by the collar of his jacket.

Dimitri shoved him to a nearby chair, his attire ripped and dirty. His face bloody and swollen.

Dominic gasped at who it was.

Adam VanCamp!

"

Dimitri what is the meaning of this?" Dominic shocked looked at him.

Breathing heavily he looked at Dominic straightening out his jacket, wiping his jaw and dusting off the little filth from his coat.

"This bastard has something to tell you," he pointed breathing heavily.

Tossed in the chair, he gave Dimitri a dirty look.

"Speak, or I will make you speak you bloody bastard." Dimitri inched closer with fist closed ready for another round of blows with Adam.

Holding up his hands, he caved sitting up straight. he spoke.

Dominic stood and listened in shock to the heartless plot between him and Hannah. His rage was at its peak. All just poured out so fast he barely got a grip of the last words. It wasn't Hannah that was pregnant.

It was Emilia.

With a murderous glare in his eyes, he lunged for Adam grabbing him by his coat and connected a blow to his face toppling him to the ground. Before he could continue, Dimitri grabbed him.

"You better pray that nothing happens to Emilia, because as God is my witness when I'm done with you, your bloody bloating body will have to be picked out of the Thames." his rage had him breathless and in tears.

Another tap at the door had Bufford walking quickly to the foyer. After a short while, he appeared at the doorframe with a burly tall man.

Bufford entered after and stood beside him.

Dominic quickly turned his back to control his rage and wipe his eyes. He turned to looked at the man with a questioning gaze, then looked at Adam still on the floor.

"M'lord, I present to you Laird Ferguson" Bufford looked forward, then continued.

"Lady Emilia's grandfather"

Immediately Dominic's face changed.

Dimitri quickly excused himself dragging Adam out into the foyer with him.

For a while, they stood looking at each other.

Dominic spoke quickly.

"Please, do sit" Dominic gestured to the only chair not toppled over in his scuffle with Adam.

Sitting down, Ferguson looked at Dominic and scoffed.

"From the looks of ye laddie, I see ma granddaughter has done a number on your heart,"

"My Emilia carries that same look," he said.

Something in Dominic's eyes came to life when he mentioned her name.

A wash of emotion and relief came over him. Letting out a deep breath he did not know he held for so long, he closed his eyes giving thanks to God she was alive and well.

Ferguson let out a laughter watching Dominic let out his breath running his hands thru his head.

"How is she? I must see her." Dominic pleaded anxiously.

Ferguson smiled faintly holding his hand up to calm Dominic's worried look.

"She is not well lad, she weeps, barely eats and is frail," Ferguson croaked.

Dominic looked away in shame because in part he was to blame for all what happened..

"She must eat it is not good for the....." Dominic stopped.

Looking into Ferguson's face, he swallowed hard and he sat straight. He had to tell him how much he loved his granddaughter, their child and his desire to marry her regardless of what anyone says.

"M'lord, Emilia and I are very much in love. She.." Ferguson stopped him before he could finish.

"I know lad about the bairn, and how much you love her is very clear. My question to you lad is how far are ye willing to go to fight for that love." Ferguson's stern look met Dominic's eyes.

"To the depths of hell if that's what it takes," Dominic returned that glare.

"Very good then, I believe ye have a long journey. Go bring my granddaughter home," Ferguson stood.

Before Dominic could say another word, Ferguson walked closer to him.

"Donna worry about my son I will handle him."

"I am not worried about the Duke, M'lord, I am worried about your granddaughter. She will not come willingly. She is head strong and very willful." Dominic looked at Ferguson.

With an amused look at Dominic, he stood before him.

"I've never known a McAllister to give up on what he wanted. Where is that McAllister blood in ye lad? Ian McAllister's blood if I'm not mistaken."

Dominic smiled and looked away. His great-grandfather always got what he wanted. Not too surprised that Ferguson knew, he was well known. But, the fact that it was pointed out that he was just like his great-grandfather a word repeated so much by his mother he sort of forgot it when she passed. Ferguson was right. He must fight for what he wanted.

Dominic stood and listened to Ferguson and together they devised a plan.

*****

Victory was on her side she mused. Shocked she opened the letter Dominic sent to her. He was off to London to get their marriage contract done and pertain to other business. He will be back in 5 days time. She was to organize an engagement party all was to be invited. Ecstatic with excitement she twirled in glee. This day could not get any better. After hearing that Emilia had left with Adam it was the best news yet. Quickly she went into the preparations for the affair. According to Dominic it had to be the affair of the season none could miss.

Chapter 22

The lush countryside from the window looked bleak. The free will and spirited abandon she once possessed was slowly slipping from her. She sat by the large window in her grandfather's library ever so often looking for a book to read.

Turning away Sarah with the large tray of food after just keeping the apple, she picked off of it. She twirled it around before lifting it to her mouth and taking a bite. The nausea and queasiness did not make it any easier for her to eat.

She watched as the clouds darkened the morning sky. Slowly the sprinkle of rain could be heard. Her mind wandered with the day it rained when she and Dominic ran free and enjoyed the feel of the rain on them.

Lifting her knees to her chest and hugging them, her emotions got the best of her and she cried.

Dashing away a tear, she stood and walked over to put the book she had in her hands away.

******

Sarah immediately walked and answered the hard knock at the door.

Blue eyes looked angrily at Sarah. Stark shock was on her face with a mixture of sheer fright and relief.

She had pulled him into the kitchen away from the halls.

"I'm waiting Sarah, why did you not tell me she was pregnant?" He scowled.

Nervously she twirled the hem of skirts .

"I wanted to m'lord but I feared what would happen if such news got out" she whispered nervously.

"So you decided to follow her days away from her home putting your lives and my unborn childs' at risk?" He breathed.

She looked sadly into his angry gaze,and tried to explain.

Lifting his hand up not wanting to hear anymore his eyes softened.

"Where is she?" He begged.

"In the library" Sarah smiled with relief and tears in her eyes.

*****

She stood back eyeing the book she wanted on the third shelf. All of the bookcases were so high she blew a deep breath. Pulling a small stepladder close she climbed to the very last step. A bit miffed at her short stature she barely touched the third case standing on her toes she stretched. Her balance a little of the ladder began to shake and gave way beneath her. The soft scream escaped her lungs as she fell back grappling for the bookcase. Sheer fright caught in her throat and she dropped.

Strong arms caught her fast in mid air. Her breath lodged in her throat.

She was face to face with Dominic.

******

He stood quietly and watched as she stretched and hopped to get the book on the shelf. Her attempt was cut short when she lost her footing and the stair toppled beneath her.

Fright lodged in his chest as she fell back.

Quickly he walked closer just in time to catch her. His heart raced with her scream.

She fell into his arms.

Face to face, their heavy breathing mingled. He held her in his arms, content to hold her this close again.

"Hello, beautiful," he whispered to her.

He held her gaze for a while. She slowly looked down. His warmth and nearness kindled a desire in her. Her voice was sweet and soft.

"You can put me down, now m'lord."

"What if I do not want to put you down?" His voice was barely a whisper.

Her heart quickened. She swallowed hard watching him gaze at her.

"You cannot hold me like this forever. Eventually you will have to let me go," her voice whispered with sad resignation in her voice.

Dark seductive stormy blue eyes held hers in place.

"I will never let you go," he squeezed her close.

The pleading look in her eyes did not waver. His resolve softened and reluctantly he let her down. The pull of his stare and his closeness pinned her in place.

Her heart clamored in her chest and roared in her ears as he caressed her cheek. He tilted her chin up, gently placing his lips on hers.

His kiss deepened and she immediately pulled away.

She looked away from his hungry gaze.

"Why are you hear?" she lowered her eyes.

"I've come to take you back home." He looked at her.

She shook her head and looked up at him.

"I can't go back."

Her refusal fell on deaf ear.

"You must, Emilia." he breathed.

"I am not going anywhere," she said in a defiant tone. "I don't have any intentions of ever returning." Her eyes held his for a while bracing herself for his anger.

She put distance between them standing behind her grandfather's desk.

She could see the muscles twitch in his jaw.

His piercing gaze held hers as he braced his hands on the table and leaned forward.

"You are returning it is not up for discussion or debate," he warned.

He continued, "You either go willingly or I drag you gagged and bound, your choice."

"You wouldn't dare" she recoiled trembling.

"Do not tempt me." His icy cool glare stared deep into her eyes.

With an upturned chin, she defiantly replied.

"Fine," Her eyes glistened with unshed tears.

"I will just leave again, and the next time I can assure you, you will never see me again." she choked furiously between a sob.

Before she finished her words, he quickly grabbed her by the arm and pulled her close.

"You will do no such thing," he hissed heavily.

His jaw clenched as he stared down into her triumphant glare knowing she hit a nerve.

He watched astonished at how her eyes darkened to a violent green with her feral gaze. Her furious struggle to break free of him surprised and amused him.

"Let me go!" she pushed at his chest with her other hand. He held her in a vice grip she could not get away from.

He yanked her close staring into daggers.

"Not until you get that absurd thought of leaving out of your head"

Emilia glared up at him as he towered over her.

"Fine then, tell me M'lord, how will the arrangement work? Will you be coming to my bed in the wee hours of the morning to have me at your will? Or set me up as your mistress."

Astonished, he watched and listened to her verbally lash out at him.

She continued watching his jaw clench at her goading words.

"Or should I writhe beneath you like some wanton whore while Lady Hannah has bloated like a cow after having a brew of your legitimate offspring?...."

"Enough!" He yelled letting her go before he turned his back on her. Closing his eyes he gathered himself. Breathing in deeply he tried to calm his anger.

"What is the matter M'lord is the truth too harsh for you." She goaded.

He swirled to look into gleaming emerald daggers that held so much anger and hurt. She backed away with a whimper as he walked her up to the bookcase with his dangerous glare.

His eyes never left hers.

"The truth is, you belong to me"

"The truth is, I will never let you go"

"The truth is, I will most definitely have you at my will beneath me, writhing with desire."

Her eyes widened with his words.

"The truth Emilia is I will not have the mother of my child putting herself at risk gallivanting across the country in such a state." he croaked.

He hit home.

Her skin turned dangerously pale.

A silence fell between them.

"You know" her lips quivered.

She frantically began to shake beneath his stare.

"You were never going to tell me, were you?." he croaked.

She looked away from him.

She let out a cry as he slammed his fists into the bookshelf at her side.

"Answer me!" his voice was dangerously low.

"No! I was never going to tell you," She cried out.

Anguished and hurt she pushed at him out of his grasp she turned to face him and his anger head on.

"I am not going to bring my baby into this world to be a bastard and the talk of the ton. He doesn't deserve it."

This delicate girl before him was surely going to put up a bold fight. a true spitfire and lioness protecting what was hers.

"You are not going to put us through that, even if I have to marry the first rake I see that can take me out of this hell I'm living in...I will," she fumed crying.

Fascinated with the glittering rage in her eyes, she was beautiful.

"Alas the petite rose strikes with her thorns," He shook his head with an icy smile at what she was screaming.

"You cannot crave a rose, if you cannot handle its thorns," she snapped.

Her heart stammered as his icy smile turned dangerous, with a blink of an eye he scooped her up in to his arms and walked over to the nearby leather couch and he lightly tossed her down. She watched his eyes dangerous and seductively burn into hers.

Breathless she scrambled back as he removed his coat, his cravat then his shirt brandishing male masculinity that was gorgeous and powerful.

Immediately and effortlessly, he snaked her ankle and like a feather, she was pulled beneath him.

He lay above her looking into her eyes.

"There are painful thorns on every rose, Emilia. But, there is only one rose worth the risk of getting pricked when touched...and that's you."

He claimed her lips and she gave no resistance.

She trembled beneath his body and he felt her shudder with the touch of his strong hands caressing her.

Her heart quickened as she felt him undo his breeches and his warmth cradled between her thighs. She tried to push at him as he violently pulled her underwear down. But she melted at the feel of his thickness entering her. He pushed forward filling her. Her eyes never left his. He marveled at how they slightly glazed over with lust and her body trembled beneath him.

"You are mine," he whispered holding her gaze.

Her eyes were red from tears threatening to fall again.

"But you will never be mine." she whispered.

Her tears fell freely as he looked down at her. His words tightened with her words. He buried his face in her neck wanting to quiet her cries but not knowing how.

After some time spent and sated she sat silently at the other end of the chair, his outstretched legs on the couch.

His eyes swept over her body, it felt different when he held her.

Her hair soft brown ringlets spiraled down her back. It formed as a curtain hiding her face.

He wanted to say so much but when he reached for her, she pulled away.

If she only knew the agony she put him through when she left and his anger towards her for not telling him or confiding in him about being pregnant. She was willing to leave him and say nothing about their child.

His heir!

But, that was behind them now. He needed to get her back home. Home! He thought.

A place she detested but needed to be for the well-being of their unborn child.

******

She sat before the mirror watching Sarah diligently comb her hair. The girl that stared back at her was unknown to her. Her bosoms slightly fuller and her waist slightly widening with her pregnancy.

Although not obvious yet, but soon it will be. How was she to explain her affair with Dominic to her uncle? The ton would have a field day with her demise. She will not endure it. She will find a way eventually to sneak away. Maybe find passage to America or another country. Wherever she can go to get far from Dominic. She would not be able to bare it watching him marry Hannah.

Yes, he was marrying Hannah because she was to wed that black-guard of VanCamp after all. According to Dominic, Adam is under the impression she is away visiting a sick cousin.

She began to cry.

She couldn't do this.

Sarah quickly turned her around facing her she begged her not to cry.

After a while of consoling from her good friend, she sat up straight dashed away her tears and accepted what was to be her fate from now until she could escape again.

Chapter 23

He looked at her. Her cool visage was remarkable, dainty and it unnerved him. Just hours ago he dreaded the thought of having to throw her over his shoulders, hissing and scratching like a cat to leave Dunkirk Manor. But, to his surprise she was dressed and ready with Sarah by her side.

She did not budge or show any sign of expression when he mentioned they would be going back so soon.

Not a word was exchanged between them or a look. Breathing heavily he leaned closer to his side of the seat praying for this torture to end.

He could not stand her silence!!!

It had been two days since they had returned and Dominic left her with her family. She sat quietly during breakfast listening to her grandfather who had just arrived from London on important business.

She was crestfallen to hear that tonight would be Dominic and Lady Hannah's engagement party and to her utter shock her family was invited. She wanted to scream and kick something.

Her thoughts were broken by Jeoffry entering and announcing the arrival of a package and letter for Emilia.

Surprised at what it could be she stood and walked towards Jeoffry with smile. He gently handed her the letter.

"Gertrude has placed your box on your bed."

Puzzled she nodded her head.

She looked down at the letter with the elegant handwritten initial A.V.

Adam VanCamp

Her heart sank she hadn't thought of him since she arrived. So much has happened she didn't remember he was away.

Slowly she opened the letter less anxious to read it contents.

Dear Emilia,I hope this letter finds you in good health. Please excuse my absence, for I have been very tied up with business matters. I will be arriving later this evening to attend Lord McAllister's and Lady Hannah's engagement party. If you do not mind, I have taken the liberty in sending you a gown to wear. When I saw it, I thought of you and how absolutely breathtaking you will look in it. Again, forgive my delay.I will see you soon,Lord EversAdam

Breathing deeply she folded it.

"Emilia dear what does it say?" Her aunt asked.

Turning she looked at the prying eyes at the table.

"It is a letter from Lord Evers, he will be joining us at the engage-ment party. He ...sent a gown for me to wear."

With a giggle and a clap, her aunt cheerfully stood from her chair and walked towards her.

"That is wonderful, mon cher," she beamed.

With a blink of an eye, her aunt squeezed her in a loving embrace before holding her hands and pulling her towards the hall up the stairs to her room.

She stood quietly next to Gertrude as her aunt cooed and awed at the gown pulled out of the box.

And indeed it was breathtaking. It was a beautiful elegant green gown, the bodice laced with an exquisite beading design.

It was divine her aunt gasped.

It was a package complete from head to toe.

Slippers, gloves, pearls and all. Fit for a princess a card read.

She went through the motions of being fixed up and dressed. The whole time her heart and soul was somewhere else slowly but surely dying.

The gasps that came from her aunt, Gertrude and Sarah when they finished told her much more than what she felt looking at herself in the mirror.

She was gorgeous.

She did not recognize the girl before her.

They ushered her out of the room and down the stairs to greet her grandfather and uncle and off they went.

~*~*~*~*~

He stood and greeted one by one each guest as they all came close to give him well wishes. Deep down he knew very well that each word from their lips lacked sincerity.

He eyed Hannah beside him doing the same ever so often he mustered up a handsome smile to her coquettish grin.

His eyes flitted lightly to the familiar faces entering the hall. Slowly guests fanned out and parted a path for them to enter, and as he suspected all eyes were on her.

An alluring beauty stood before him and his heart thumped so hard at the sight of her.

He cooley greeted her uncle, aunt and grandfather then her. Trying not to show any emotion, he bent his head to her hand and kissed it lightly.

Beneath hooded eyes, he could see her eyes sadden and her cheeks flush a light pink before standing straight and greeting the rest of the guests.

Drinks and dancing started. He watched beneath hooded eyes beside Hannah, how Emilia sat quietly watching the dancers. He sipped gingerly at his wine and continued his small talk with the surrounding men.

As the music slowed, Hannah urged him giving him the cue that it was time for a speech. All candidly stood smiling and laughing as she pulled him to the middle of the floor.

He smiled chuckling with outstretched hands waiting for the cheers to lower.

He stood for a while lowering his head giving some thought to what he was going to say.

Clearing his throat, he gave another smile.

He gave a quick turn to acknowledge everyone before him.

"I guess I should start off by giving a speech of how we met." he smiled.

The chuckles followed.

He eyed Hannah that coquettishly shook her head.

He boyishly grinned and ducked his head.

"I can most definitely tell you all that the day I met her she took my breath away."

The awes and coos followed.

"When I am with her nothing else in this world exists. All time stops."

He lowered his head.

"I can assure you there are times when she infuriated me with her stubbornness and rebellious ways but just the look of her softens me to the core."

"She is free willed, spirited and very beautiful."

Between hooded eyes, he took a quick glance towards Emilia. She immediately lowered her eyes and tried to step back but she couldn't.

"I can't imagine my life without her,"

He turned towards Hannah and watched her smile fade and slip from confusion to horror following gasps from onlookers watched Dominic walk over to Emilia.

He held out his hand.

She looked up to him with confused beautiful eyes. Her aunt gave her a gentle push before smiling happily at them both.

Nervous and shaky she followed him to the center of the hall.

Wide eyes filled with shock stared at them.

His eyes held hers and they were filled with so much passion and love.

"I want all of you to know that this delicate beauty before me is who I am speaking of,"

He pulled her cold hands towards his lips kissing them both.

Nervously she looked around before looking up into his eyes.

"Dominic, what are you doing?" her lips quivered.

He looked at everyone with shocked gazes.

"I want all of you to know it was never my intention to marry Lady Hannah. I cannot marry someone as conniving, evil and manipulative as she," he looked straight at her.

She stomped furiously.

"All of you take a good look at the scheming snake that nearly ruined any chances of me being happy. She was plotting with her lover to separate Emilia and I, then pass off Emilia's child as her own."

Gasps and whispers followed immediately as they began to step away from Hannah with disappointing stares.

Astonished by that Emilia looked into his eyes for the truth and it was clear as day it was.

"I did all of this for you all to see the length I am willing to go. To fight for the love of my life and our unborn child."

He stared deep into her eyes.

He gently caressed her cheek.

"I told you before I will never let you go." he whispered.

Her heart raced in her chest as she watched him bend on one knee before her. He pulled a small box out of his pocket took the shiny ring and presented it to her.

"Emilia Claire Westham, will you do me the honor making me the happiest man on earth by becoming my wife."

Her hands trembled and covered her lips, tears fell freely clouding her vision. She turned to look at her uncle shockingly finding seven familiar faces: Helmsley, Bufford, Jeoffrey, Sarah, Gertrude and Dimitri. All of them beaming with joy and nodding their approval.

She turned to look down into a gorgeous wicked smile.

With a brief giggle and sob, she said. "Yes."

With a smile, he lifted her in to his arms and twirled her around. To their surprise, claps and hurrahs followed.

He set her down gently and looked deep into her eyes.

He claimed her lips and kissed her with an intense need.

"I love you." She whispered.

His seductive smile warmed her to the core.

"I love you, more."

After such a display, they were sure they would be exiled and casted out of the posh aristocratic society. However, to their surprise they were the most sought after to attend soirees and feasts.

Their wedding was performed immediately by a special license obtained by her grandfather. It was a wedding in its entire splendor and all witnessed the union of two souls destined to be together forever.

Epilogue

The soft patter of his heart warmed hers but, as odd as it was its rhythm matched hers. They lay together in a tangled abandonment of sheets and limbs resting after their most luxurious lovemaking.

She listened quietly to all what had happened while she was gone. How with the help of her grandfather he did it all. How Dimitri discovered Adam and Hannah's plot to separate them. And that it was he who sent her the dress. He did all of it for her.

His face was buried in her hair he marveled in its softness and sweet scent.

He grasped her hand and folded his fingers gently between hers. He leaned on his elbow and looked down at her. Her eyes twinkled with such a smile it was contagious that he could do nothing but smile back with a wide gorgeous grin.

"I still cannot believe this is not a dream," she caressed his face and watched him turn his lips to kiss the inside of her palm.

"I can assure you it is not," he shook his head and laughed.

"I... have a confession to make," She whispered softly and giggled at his now serious glare.

She lowered her gaze and focused on their intertwined fingers.

"I cherish the first kiss you gave me," she whispered.

Puzzled he stared into her eyes they held his gaze with such love.

"You little minx, I thought you had fallen asleep," he gave an amusing look.

Shaking her head, she bit her lip with a shy smile.

"I felt so ashamed to look at you after such a bold wanton move, I feigned sleep," She smiled shyly at him.

His amusing grin made her hide her enflamed cheeks.

"And I have a confession to make as well," He trailed his fingers softly along her lips.

Her eyes were fixed on his.

"That was the night I realized that I was falling deeply in love with you."

Her eye sparkled with her smile at such a confession.

She pulled him close for a kiss.

After a while, she turned to lean on her elbow and looked at him.

"Will you still want me even if I have grown big and bloated like a cow?" Her eyes looked to him with a pouty stare.

He chuckled with a boisterous laugh.

Laying her back on her pillow, he smiled down at her.

"What makes you think I will not," he searched her eyes.

Her eyes lowered and she nervously licked her lips.

"How would we be able to...?" She hesitated before looking at him.

"To make love?" He grinned teasingly.

He stared down into her eyes with such a salacious gaze that her heart quivered.

He kissed her lips.

"I can tell you...or...I can show you..." he gave a devilish smile.

With a gasp, her eyes watched him slowly trail kisses down her body.

"My lord, your wicked." she gasped.

His enticing smile promised something just as that and much more.

"And you, my beauty are delicious," he gave sexy grin.

With that said, London's most gorgeous rake swept his beautiful rose into the clouds.

Lightning Source UK Ltd.
Milton Keynes UK
UKHW020440211122
412554UK00016B/799